A PARTY TO MURDER

A PARTY TO MURDER

Michael Underwood

St. Martin's Press
New York

Library of Congress Cataloging in Publication Data

Underwood, Michael, 1916-
  A party to murder.

  I. Title.
PR6055.V3P3   1983   823'.914   83-17676
ISBN 0-312-59768-1

First published in Great Britain in 1983 by Macmillan London Limited

First U.S. Edition

10 9 8 7 6 5 4 3 2 1

CHAPTER ONE

'I'm afraid Charles is going to be terribly disappointed,' Tom Hunsey said in the tone of nervous relish he used for relaying the choicer bits of office gossip.

This, it was later agreed, was the understatement of the year. Charles Buck was not only disappointed, he was livid. Moreover he took no trouble to hide his bitterness and resentment at the appointment which had been made over his head and which he had been sure would be his. And when later Murray Riston arrived to take up his post as Chief Prosecuting Solicitor for Grainfield and its surrounding area, Buck displayed a personal hostility toward him which even those who thought he had been treated shabbily found embarrassing.

'Heard the news?' Tom Hunsey enquired eagerly as he made his rounds. 'Murray Riston's to be our new boss . . . Yes, Murray . . . Bit of a surprise, isn't it? . . . Must say I never expected him to show his face back here again . . . Mind you, he's able enough and I personally always got on with him all right, *but* . . .'

At this point, Hunsey would wait for the recipient of his tidings to give vent to an opinion of his own which he could embellish on arrival at his next port of call.

'Peter thinks there'll be one or two resignations,' he had said without any justification. In fact Peter Shoreham, when drawn on the subject, had merely remarked that he expected

5

the appointment to be a nine days' wonder and thereafter to be accepted without fuss.

But it was a room at the end of the second floor corridor that Hunsey approached with an increased tingling of anticipation.

'Hello, Caroline,' he said as he sidled in, closing the door behind him and casting her an expectant look. 'Wondered if you'd heard the news?'

Caroline Allard looked up from the file she had been reading and frowned. Tom Hunsey's interruptions were as frequent as they were usually irksome.

'What news?' she asked without enthusiasm. Like most of his colleagues she regarded Hunsey with a mixture of amused tolerance and contempt. Though he was twenty years her senior and had been on the prosecuting solicitor's staff for three times as long as she, he was not a person to command her respect, nor indeed that of most of the staff, who were divided in opinion as to whether he was deliberately malicious or just naturally devious.

'Our new boss,' he said, cocking his head on one side and fixing her with a tentative smile. 'The appointment's been made. I heard just now from Edward's secretary.'

Miss Vincent, secretary to Edward Patching, the retiring Chief Prosecuting Solicitor, was the source of much of Tom Hunsey's gossip. He flattered and amused her and was rewarded with titbits of inside information.

'You're obviously dying to tell me so get on with it,' Caroline said tartly when Hunsey went on watching her with the same small tentative smile.

'Have a guess!'

'I've no idea and I've got a lot of work to do . . .'

'It's Murray,' he said quickly, avid for her reaction.

'Murray Riston?' Her tone was incredulous.

'None other. Thought you'd be surprised. Mind you, he's capable enough, but that isn't everything as we all

6

know . . .' His voice trailed away hopefully, but Caroline Allard showed no inclination to make further comment. Her long equine face became a study of blankness.

'Well I must get on,' she said at length in a stony voice, as she bent over the file she had been reading.

'Afraid the news knocked poor Caroline for six,' Tom Hunsey said to Trevor Williams in the next room. 'I must say I don't know how he has the nerve to come back after what he did to her. To be seduced and discarded and then have your lover return as your boss, well!'

Meanwhile on the floor below in a large room with bay windows overlooking two aspects of the garden, Edward Patching was talking to his deputy, Charles Buck.

'I know you're upset, Charles, and believe me I really did give you my backing with the committee, but they were obviously determined to bring in someone from outside.'

Charles Buck let out an uncompromising snort. 'Is that what Riston's supposed to be? Someone from outside! How he had the bloody nerve to apply, I'll never know.' He was silent for a moment while he marshalled his savage thoughts. 'When one recalls the circumstances in which he left here five years ago. There was that distinctly fishy business involving Rex Kline and I'm sure Riston knew more about that than he ever let on. And when he went and married Kline's daughter I was certain of it. Not to mention the shameful way he treated Caroline Allard . . .' His voice trailed angrily away.

Edward Patching observed him with a gravely judicial air. 'I know, I know, but you must suppress your personal feelings for the sake of the team. Vendettas are so destructive.'

'It's not a question of a vendetta, but of having to work with somebody for whom you have no respect.'

'Murray's able enough.'

'So I'm always being told! What about my abilities at the age of fifty-five? I suppose it's taken for granted that I'll go on

7

being the loyal deputy C.P.S. until I retire.'

Charles Buck had the build and forceful air of a front-line rugger forward. He tended to have favourites among the legal staff and was consequently disliked (and feared) by those who didn't enjoy his patronage.

'Wait till Peggy hears, she'll go off like a land mine,' he remarked morosely, referring to his wife who was not unlike a rugger forward herself. 'She could never stand the little twerp.'

Edward Patching pursed his lips in disapproval. He had never cared for Peggy Buck and even less so after learning of the scathing comments she made about him on the occasion of his divorce four years before. After thirty years of faithful marriage he had suddenly at the age of fifty-eight had a passionate affair with a girl from a typing agency who had come to him as a temporary secretary. His wife had promptly divorced him and extracted every penny she could in alimony. He had thereafter married Alison, the girl in question, who was thirty years his junior and who was now unenthusiastically facing the prospect of being the wife of a retired prosecuting solicitor living on a reduced pension. It was not what she had envisaged when she had married him.

Patching glanced at his watch.

'I'm afraid I must ask you, Charles, to go and lick your wounds elsewhere as I have someone coming from the *Gazette* to interview me in a few minutes time.'

Edward Patching felt sorry for his deputy, but not that sorry. Indeed, despite what he had just said to his face, he had done nothing whatsoever to espouse his cause with the committee of appointment.

'I suppose the news of Riston's appointment is all round the office by now,' Buck remarked in a still bitter voice.

'I imagine Tom Hunsey will have seen to that,' Patching said in a tone that did nothing to soothe his deputy's feelings.

With Charles Buck's departure, he went over to one of the

8

bay windows and gazed out. One of the council's gardeners was sweeping up leaves and conveying them to a rather depressed-looking bonfire on the farther side. The original intention had been that the Prosecuting Solicitor's staff should move into part of the new police headquarters complex which had been built about four miles outside Grainfield, whose ancient abbey and narrow arcaded streets provided a major tourist attraction and had over the years caused the various elements of the municipal authority to move outside the town's perimeter where they could expand more comfortably. However, when the police building was finally completed two years late and a million pounds over its estimated cost, it was realised it couldn't accommodate any hangers-on.

Fortunately, from the housing department's point of view, there was Grainfield Manor lying empty, a large Victorian house which had been on the market for several years. It was totally unsuited to any form of modern living and even less so to office use. Nevertheless, Edward Patching and his staff were moved there, it being only a mile and a half down the road from police headquarters.

The C.P.S. and his deputy had pleasant enough rooms, but the registry was situated in what had been the kitchen and a number of junior staff were located in pokey rooms at the top of the house where water tanks rumbled and gurgled the day long.

'Just like working alongside a giant with the colly-wobbles,' someone had remarked plaintively.

Patching sighed. It would be his view for only another few weeks. Then it would be Murray Riston's. The intercom on his desk gave an eager buzz and his secretary informed him that Miss Gillian Osprey from the *Gazette* had arrived.

He had been interviewed on a number of previous occasions, invariably by brash young men or alarmingly confident young women, who showed scant respect for his position or for his mature years. He was surprised, therefore, when his door opened and a woman in her mid-forties strode in looking as if she had come straight off a golf course. She had severely cut iron grey hair and a complexion which matched the gingery brown tweed trouser suit she was wearing.

'Mr Patching? I'm Gillian Osprey,' she said, thrusting out her hand. 'We've not met before.'

Thrown off balance by such a forthright approach, Edward Patching could only murmur, 'Er . . . no, we haven't. Won't you sit down. Can I offer you a cup of tea?'

But, as if to show her contempt for any pleasantries, Gillian Osprey had gone over to the window and was gazing out with a heavy frown.

'So this is where all the big decisions are made,' she said, suddenly swinging round and fixing him with a concentrated stare.

The C.P.S. gave a nervous laugh. 'I don't think I'd quite describe my job that way.'

'Why not?'

'Because it isn't. But do come and sit down, Miss Osprey.'

'If you want to be formal, it's Mrs Osprey.' She saw him quickly glance at her left hand and went on, 'I've been divorced twice and don't wear a wedding ring any longer. But to return to what you were saying, why do you seek to play down your job?'

'I don't . . .'

'You make decisions affecting people's liberty, don't you? It's you who decide whether or not they should be prosecuted?'

'Ye-es.'

'Do you not consider those big decisions?'

'In one sense yes, of course . . .'

'Well, that's all I said.' She cast a baleful glance at the tape recorder she had placed on the desk between them. 'Hope that damned thing's working!' She returned her attention to the C.P.S. who shifted uneasily in his chair. 'It might help if you explained your reservations, Mr Patching,' she said severely.

'It was merely that you spoke of big decisions as though I exercised some dictator's power. In fact all the biggest decisions in the prosecuting field are made by the Director of Public Prosecutions in London. You may not be aware of it, but a whole range of serious crimes must, by regulation, be reported to his department and it is he who decides whether or not action should be taken.'

'Do you mind that?'

'It's the system.'

'But don't you find it galling not to be able to decide here in Grainfield whether, for example, somebody should be prosecuted for murder?'

'If the police have enough evidence to charge someone with murder, they do so without reference to me or to the D.P.P.'

'But the case has ultimately to go to the D.P.P?'

'Yes.'

'And you don't feel that a slight on your professional ability?'

'No.' He smiled complacently. 'Not that I wouldn't be capable of handling such a case myself. As I explained, it's the system.'

Mrs Osprey gave the tape recorder a sharp tap and glared at it.

'I understand,' she went on, 'that, as the local prosecuting solicitor, you have less discretion than the D.P.P. For example, that the D.P.P. can refuse to sanction proceedings in a case even though there may be sufficient evidence to support a charge: that he can say the public interest doesn't call for a prosecution. Whereas, provided the evidence is there and the police want a case brought in court, you have no choice but to prosecute whatever your feelings about the merits.'

Edward Patching gave a slight squirm. He was a vain man and didn't like interviewers who reminded him he was less than Godlike.

'I've always enjoyed an excellent working relationship with the police,' he said stiffly. 'If I considered a case had no merits, I'm sure I'd be able to persuade the police to see it my way.'

'But supposing you couldn't?'

'It's never arisen.'

'Is that because you know they have the whip hand and you're therefore careful to avoid confrontations?'

'Certainly not. You're suggesting I bow to the wind and am prepared to be false to my conscience.'

Mrs Osprey gave him an amused smile. 'I didn't mean to make you cross,' she said. 'Tell me about the most difficult decision you've ever had to make as Prosecuting Solicitor?'

'I'm afraid I can't possibly discuss individual cases.'

'Why not?'

'Because it'd be a breach of confidence.'

'Aren't the public who pay your salary entitled to know?'

'The fact I'm a public servant doesn't entitle the public at large to know everything that goes on in this building. After all, you'd hardly expect your solicitor to publish your private affairs to the world, would you?'

'He's paid by me and not by the taxpayer. It makes a difference.'

'The principle's the same,' Edward Patching said firmly and hoped his interviewer would change the subject. To his relief she did so.

'I understand your successor as C.P.S. has just been named. Mr Murray Riston, is that right?'

'Yes.'

'I believe he was once on the staff here?'

12

'Yes. He left about five years ago to become a deputy prosecuting solicitor in the north of England. Now he's returning.'

'A surprise appointment would you say?' Gillian Osprey said with a small sardonic smile.

Edward Patching frowned as if puzzled by the question. 'Not at all.'

'I gather the committee making the appointment has been unusually secretive in its deliberations. For example, they refused to divulge the names of the candidates they were proposing to interview.'

'I'm afraid I can't comment on that. I wasn't on the committee and played no part in its deliberations.'

'But presumably you knew that Mr Riston had applied for your job?'

'This isn't a matter I'm prepared to discuss. Moreover, it has nothing whatsoever to do with the subject of this interview.'

'I believe he's married to a local girl, Jennifer Kline,' Mrs Osprey went on as if Edward Patching hadn't spoken.

The C.P.S. nodded in an offhand manner. 'They met when he was on the staff here.'

'I expect you know Rex Kline, her father?'

'I've met him at a number of official functions,' he said coldly.

Gillian Osprey smiled to herself. Mention of Rex Kline's name could usually be guaranteed to cause a few ripples in any conversational pond. It would be her guess that he'd tried to pull a few strings to secure his son-in-law's appointment. It wouldn't be past him and there had been the odd rumour of undue influence when Murray Riston was courting his daughter. But then Rex Kline was the sort of person who spawned rumour whatever he did. He had made a fortune in property over the past decade and had become a J.P. and a man of standing in local affairs.

13

Edward Patching glanced at his watch. Gillian Osprey noticed but ignored the hint.

'Are you looking forward to your retirement?'

'Yes and no. I'll miss the work, of course, and the professional cameraderie. On the other hand, there comes a time to pass on the baton.' He gave her a complacent smile as though he had uttered a number of profundities.

'What are your particular interests outside the law?'

'Classical music and gardening,' he said as if he had been waiting for the question.

I might have guessed it, she thought. Pompous and unoriginal to the end.

'I ought to have asked you this at the beginning and got it out of the way. What's the size of your staff?'

'Legal staff, you mean?'

'Any old staff,' she replied casually.

'There's myself, my deputy and eight assistant solicitors.'

'Do you go into court yourself?'

'Virtually never. I could do, but I prefer to make myself available for meetings and conferences and not become bogged down in court in any one particular case.'

'What about your deputy?'

'He goes into court on really important cases.'

'Such as?'

'Robberies and large scale burglaries. Also rape cases and attempted murders.'

'I thought they had to be done by the D.P.P.'

'They have to be reported to him, but he usually leaves us to conduct the prosecutions. He hasn't the staff to handle everything that's referred to him.'

'It's a pretty cock-eyed system, wouldn't you agree?'

Edward Patching smiled indulgently. 'It might appear that way but I assure you it works.'

Mrs Osprey looked sceptical as she leaned forward to switch off the tape recorder. It was her view that lawyers

14

tended to be more conservative and complacent than any other section of society and Edward Patching was clearly no exception. Let him bask in his classical music and gardening! From the homework she had done before coming, she had gained the impression that he was still recovering from a particularly messy and expensive divorce.

To her the interview had been as much of a chore as she had expected. She assessed the retiring C.P.S. of Grainfield as a prototype of mediocrity, with delusions of adequacy. Beneath the impressive silvery hair nestled an atrophied brain.

At least, from all accounts, his successor sounded a livelier personality.

CHAPTER TWO

Murray and Jennifer Riston were on their way to spend a long weekend with her parents who lived about eight miles outside Grainfield. Their main purpose was to find a place of their own in the area, for Murray was due to take up his appointment in a few weeks' time. They had a short-list of possible houses and were hoping to settle on one during their visit.

Jennifer was fourteen years younger than her husband, a neat, compact girl with short, dark hair that always had a gloss to it. At forty-two Murray had a perennially boyish air. His face was round without being chubby and his hair, which was almost the same colour as his wife's, gave him a faintly tousled look even when it had just been combed.

First acquaintances came away charmed by his friendly manner, unless he had happened to take against them when he could be cold and distant. Those who knew him well were aware of the core of steel beneath the amiable exterior.

'Will you get in touch with the office while we're here?' Jennifer enquired as a signpost informed them of their nearness to Grainfield.

He shook his head. 'I suspect they'll like a bit longer to digest the news of my appointment before I actually show my face,' he said lightly.

'Who, apart from Charles Buck, might be difficult?'

'There are one or two who won't be dancing in the streets

16

over my return, but Charles is probably the only one who's hoping I'll drop dead before I arrive.'

'What about Caroline Allard?'

'What about her?'

'Wasn't she meant to be rather fond of you?'

'We went out a few times together, but that was all.'

'She's never married, has she?'

'Not as far as I know. I imagine I'd have heard if she had.' After a slight pause, he went on in a serious tone, 'Caroline never meant anything to me. I've told you that before. She belongs to my past. Don't let's think about her.'

'But you're about to become her boss.'

'I'm sure we'll both cope with the situation in a civilised way.'

'Are you going to make many changes in the office?'

'I just want to make it a more efficient and dynamic place. Edward Patching's let things drift. He's always wanted to be all things to all people, which means soft options and appeasement. Charles Buck's been the power behind the throne.' He paused before adding with a quick grin, 'God, but he must be furious about my appointment!'

'Perhaps he'll take early retirement.'

'I doubt it, not that I'd do anything to stop him. However if he wants to be bloody-minded, he'll learn it's a two-way game. He'll also learn who has the whip-hand.'

Jennifer gave a small shiver. 'I hate the thought of your running into any unpleasantness.'

'Don't worry, sweetheart, I can look after myself. I'd never have applied for the job otherwise.'

Jennifer remained silent. She knew that, provided merit was the criterion, her husband had never doubted he would be successful in his application. He was, however, the first to admit that in municipal government merit often sank to the bottom in a bran-tub of vested interests.

She and Murray had been married for four years and had a

17

three-year-old daughter named Nicola. It was a generally happy marriage in which Jennifer made most of the compromises. She knew her husband possessed a tough, ruthless streak and she avoided doing anything to provoke it. She looked forward to returning to Grainfield as Mrs Riston, not only because it meant living closer to her parents, but because she relished the social life attached to being the wife of its Chief Prosecuting Solicitor.

'A penny for your thoughts,' he said, casting her a sidelong glance.

'Just that I'm looking forward to the weekend.'

'So am I. And in a few weeks' time, this'll be home again,' he said, waving a proprietorial hand at a field of cows they happened to be passing.

At about that same moment Murray Riston was occupying the thoughts of Chief Superintendent Bernard Tarr, the officer in charge of the Grainfield division of the county police. He had been Detective Inspector Tarr when Murray had been on the prosecuting staff at Grainfield and they had worked together on many cases. Since then he had been promoted and transferred to the uniform branch and now Murray was about to return as Chief Prosecuting Solicitor for the area.

Tarr thought it a good appointment, though he was aware of the repercussions it would cause. To him, however, Murray represented efficiency and the prosecuting solicitor's office could do with a touch of that. Edward Patching had become a time-server and whatever zest for his job he might once have had seemed to have been drained out of him by his divorce. As for Charles Buck he was a mixture of school-master and sergeant-major, which might be all right in a Chief Superintendent, but was definitely not so in a deputy C.P.S. Thank heaven he, at least, hadn't been appointed.

As for the rest of the staff Tarr regarded them as ranging

18

from the mediocre to the incompetent. Among the latter was Tom Hunsey who had been there longer than anybody and who should have been kicked out years before. He was not only useless at his job, but dangerously so. In the criminal world he would have been a grass: on the C.P.S.'s staff he was an arch noser-out of scandal.

If Murray Riston had as much spunk as Tarr believed, he would lose no time in getting rid of both Buck and Hunsey. The one because he would prove to be an implacable foe, the other because he was an incompetent menace.

'Sorry I wasn't here when you arrived,' Rex Kline said heartily as he advanced across the room to embrace his daughter. Then turning to his son-in-law, he clasped him by the shoulders and exclaimed, 'the prodigal returns, eh!'

'I don't see any resemblance between Murray and the prodigal son,' Jennifer observed in a faintly reproving tone.

'I've never been one for the right quotation,' her father remarked cheerfully. 'Anyway, it's good to welcome you back to Grainfield, my lad,' he went on with a beaming smile.

'But you saw him when he was down here for the interview last week,' Jennifer said. 'Why are you addressing him as if you'd not seen him for months?'

'Because he wasn't Chief Prosecuting Solicitor the last time I saw him, that's why, Miss Bossy Boots!' her father retorted, putting an affectionate arm round her waist. 'I've got a couple of bottles of Dom Perignon on ice and we don't celebrate that way every time you come. This is a special occasion. I'll go and fetch them now.'

'Isn't it a bit early, Rex?' his wife said.

'When has it ever been too early to drink champagne?' he remarked as he headed out of the room.

'He's so thrilled about your appointment, Murray. He says it's the best thing that's happened to Grainfield since the Romans departed.'

19

Murray Riston let out a laugh. 'I can't believe anyone else regards it as an event for spectacular celebration. Indeed, I can think of some who, *pace* the Romans, will consider it the worst appointment since Caligula made his horse a consul.'

'Rubbish,' his mother-in-law said robustly, just as her husband returned to the room bearing a tray of glasses and a bottle of champagne. Murray gave her a warm smile. He always enjoyed having her rush to his defence, though nobody normally required less protection than he.

'To our new Chief Prosecuting Solicitor,' Rex Kline said, raising his glass.

'In the circumstances I shall join you and drink to myself,' Murray said with a grin.

'I have a bit of news for you both,' Kline said a few moments later, giving his wife a wink. 'No need to go looking for a house, you're going to have this one.' Delighted by the effect of his bombshell, he turned to his wife. 'I mean it, don't I, Molly?'

Molly Kline nodded. 'He's been talking about it all week. We want you to come here.'

'But where will you live?' Jennifer asked in a bewildered tone.

'I've bought a nice little modern Georgian house on the other side of Grainfield. Signed the contract yesterday. People had to sell in a hurry. Had my eye on it for some time. It's all settled.'

Jennifer glanced worriedly from her father to her mother. Her childhood had been punctuated by the upheaval of moving home, as three years was the longest her father could bear to live in one house. Her mother had often been presented with little more than a fait accompli, but uncomplainingly accepted her husband's unpredictable behaviour.

'But I could never afford to buy this place,' Murray expostulated.

'You don't have to. You can have it for a peppercorn rent for the time being. Anyway, it's not the moment to discuss such sordid details. Molly and I reckon we can be out in a month which means it'll be ready for your occupation when you take up your appointment at the end of November.' He paused and beamed at his daughter and son-in-law. 'So you see, everything's settled. Now I'll go and fetch that other bottle of champagne.'

CHAPTER THREE

Monday, November 18th, was a dank, misty day. Not that Murray Riston was particularly aware of the weather as he drove toward Grainfield Manor and his first day as Chief Prosecuting Solicitor. His mind was on the pleasantries he would exchange with those who greeted him. He was determined to show himself in his most seductive colours. Bygones were bygones as far as he was concerned and he hoped others felt the same. He realised that he couldn't expect anything approaching a warm welcome from Charles Buck, but even his sense of occasion should, at least, ensure a dignified reception.

As his car rounded a bend in the drive and the main entrance came into view he peered to see if he could recognise those waiting in the porch to greet him. He wasn't expecting a guard of honour, but at this distance he couldn't spot a single person. He parked his car in the space reserved for the C.P.S. and slowly got out, reaching for his coat and brief case on the back seat. As he advanced toward the front door, George Ives, the chief clerk, came hurrying out.

'Good morning, Mr Riston. Welcome back!'

'Thanks, George. It's good to be here again,' Murray said as they shook hands. With a small, self-deprecating smile he added, 'I was beginning to wonder if I'd come on the wrong day.'

'I'm afraid you've caught us on a really busy one,' Ives said

22

with obvious embarrassment. 'Mr Buck's at a conference at police headquarters and practically everyone else is in court.'

Murray nodded genially. He assumed that Charles Buck had probably arranged his conference at that hour deliberately to avoid having to greet him on arrival. He was determined, however, not to be ruffled by the affront.

As he and George Ives made their way up to his room on the first floor, it seemed that every door they passed remained forbiddingly closed. But suddenly a voice hailed him from behind.

'Hello there, Murray. Welcome home!'

He turned to have his hand seized and energetically pumped by Tom Hunsey.

'I was beginning to think I'd come aboard the Mary Celeste,' Murray said wryly.

'What? Oh, I see what you mean . . . yes, the place is rather deserted . . . I don't know where Charles Buck has got to.'

'I gather he's at a meeting with the police.'

Murray opened the door of his room and went in, followed by Tom Hunsey, who was apt to pursue people relentlessly while talking to them.

'I'd have thought he'd have been here to greet you,' Hunsey said, striding over to the window and looking out. 'How does it feel to be back?' he asked, swinging round and gazing at the new C.P.S. with his head cocked on one side. Without waiting for an answer, he went on, 'Expect you're planning some changes, eh?'

'Stop prattling on like an interviewer, Tom,' Murray said goodnaturedly.

'Well, I'll leave you to settle in,' Hunsey said. 'By the way, the Christmas party's fixed for two weeks tomorrow. We thought we'd make it a combined affair. A welcome to you and a farewell to Edward.' He moved with seeming reluctance toward the door. 'How's Jennifer?'

23

'She's fine.'

'I hear you've moved into your father-in-law's old house?'

'Yes.'

'How are Mr and Mrs Kline?'

'Also fine.'

Hunsey frowned and appeared to be on the verge of saying something further when he gave an abstracted nod and stalked from the room.

'Mr Hunsey doesn't change much, does he?' George Ives remarked from the door where he'd been hovering.

Murray made a slight grimace. As far as he was concerned Hunsey was a piece of dead wood who should have been axed several years ago. He had once had a good brain and had been an able lawyer, but his intellectual processes had degenerated so that he was now unable to take the simplest decisions and was constantly plaguing his colleagues with questions he couldn't be bothered to answer for himself.

'Give me half an hour to sort myself out, George, then come back and brief me on anything I ought to know about,' Murray said after a silence during which he stared moodily around him.

Each of them was aware that this should by rights have been Charles Buck's task, but Ives showed no surprise.

'Certainly, sir,' he said with the air of a perfect butler, as he retired, closing the door behind him.

For a while Murray continued standing by his desk, gazing about him as if unsure what he should do next. His homecoming hadn't been quite as he had envisaged it. Or had it?

A discreet knock on the door that led to his secretary's office brought him out of his reverie. A short, bespectacled woman of middle years came into the room.

'I'm Miss Vincent, Mr Riston. I've been Mr Patching's secretary for the last two years.'

Murray gave her a warm smile as he held out his hand. 'I'm

happy to meet you, Miss Vincent. I hope you'll find me as easy to work for as I'm sure Mr Patching was.'

As she was to remark to a friend that evening, 'I don't know where all the rumours about him come from. He couldn't be friendlier. Mr Patching was all right, but Mr Riston's got real charm.'

It was toward the end of the morning that Tom Hunsey was passing the C.P.S.'s door when he heard Charles Buck's voice within. Having first made sure that he was not being observed, he veered toward the door and listened.

'If I could afford to retire now, I would, but I can't,' he heard Charles Buck say. 'Nor have I any hope of another appointment. It's as well, therefore, that we should understand one another. I don't pretend to like you and I'm astonished you had the nerve to apply for this job. And I'm not just referring to your callous treatment of Caroline Allard . . .'

Hunsey put his head closer to the door to try and catch Murray Riston's response, but could only hear the murmur of his voice.

'Spare me your soft words!' he heard Buck break in scornfully. 'Let's just accept that we're stuck with one another. I've no doubt that you'd like to be rid of me, but even you can't always have everything your own way.'

A door opened in the distance and Hunsey straightened up and reluctantly moved away. Almost immediately Peter Shoreham came round a corner.

'Hello, Peter, had a chance to see our new boss yet?'

Shoreham shook his head. 'I've only just come back from court. I gather he's going to tour the building this afternoon and say hello to everyone.' Observing Hunsey's expression he added, 'Don't say I've actually managed to tell *you* something, Tom!'

'Where'd you hear that?' Hunsey asked, ignoring the note of mockery in his colleague's voice.

25

'Caroline told me.'

'Caroline? Has she seen Murray already?'

'I've no idea.'

'I wonder what they'll say to one another,' Hunsey remarked, rubbing his hands together with nervous relish. Nodding his head in the direction of the C.P.S.'s door he added, 'I think I heard Charles's voice when I passed just now.'

'Seems reasonable he should talk to his deputy,' Shoreham replied blandly.

'Come off it, Peter! You know you're just as intrigued as I am.' He rubbed his hands together again. 'Murray and Charles are never going to hit it off together. If I told you some of the things Charles has said . . .'

'I don't want to hear them,' Shoreham broke in strenuously. 'Murray's our new C.P.S. and it's Charles's duty to give him all the support he needs. Our office is too small for personal feuding. It doesn't help anybody and, in the end, destroys morale. It's probably too much to hope they'll be friends, but I trust for all our sakes they won't let their personal feelings toward each other affect the running of the office.'

Having thus delivered himself, Peter Shoreham turned abruptly on his heel, leaving Tom Hunsey staring after him with a surprised expression.

Hunsey's mind went back to what he had heard through the door before Shoreham's untimely appearance. The particular mention of Caroline Allard had excited his interest and given him food for thought.

After thirty years in the C.P.S.'s office his life would be impossibly dull without his extra-mural interests.

His addiction to ferreting out gossip had, however, dulled his awareness that it could be a dangerous pursuit.

CHAPTER FOUR

Caroline Allard threw down her pen and pushed her chair back from the desk. It was no good, she just couldn't concentrate and that annoyed her. Until now she had believed she had her emotions under control and would be able to cope with Murray's return as C.P.S.

After all, five years had gone by since his departure and she had not seen him in the interval. Indeed, she had sought to blot him out of her mind and this had been made easier by their geographical separation. Life would have been intolerable if he had remained at Grainfield after what had happened between them. As it was his posting to the north of England had been providential from her point of view.

She now realised, and deep in her heart had known all along, that their affair had meant far more to her than to him. She had been thirty and still a virgin when he had seduced her. She had been aware of his reputation with girls, but had persuaded herself that she was different and someone special to him. Her initial caution had merely served to increase his protestations of love. They were made for one another, he had declared, and she had believed him. Believed him because she wanted to. And then instead of a proposal of marriage had come evasion and deceit. This took the form of excuses for not seeing her so often. Excuses which he took less and less trouble to make plausible.

Others saw what was happening, they always did, but she

had refused to read the signs. After all, she'd always regarded herself as a practical woman with the in-built caution bred of a lawyer's training. Moreover she firmly believed that her head would never let her heart control her destiny. How wrong she had been and with what devastating results to her morale!

For a whole year she had privately moped. Her work had suffered and she had become listless and uninterested in life. It had been like a bereavement. But eventually the pall had lifted and she had regained her normal resilience. Murray had been exorcised and was no longer in her system.

When news of his return to Grainfield had first reached her, she had been startled, then angry. How dare he come back as if nothing had ever happened! Did he imagine she had forgiven and forgotten what had passed between them? Did he think it was now no more than a pleasant but fading memory? Was he not aware of the wounds he would be reopening?

Then as the weeks before his arrival went by, she had had time to come to terms with the situation. She had determined not to allow bitterness or resentment to poison her life, not for his sake, heaven knows, but for her own.

But now he was here, actually in the building. Moreover, any moment he would open her door and greet her as one of his staff.

She closed her eyes, willing herself to behave with composure when that happened.

She got up from her desk and went over to a cupboard in which she kept a number of case files as well as a reserve cardigan and a spare pair of shoes. She stared into the cupboard and tried to still her emotions as the urge to flee her room and hide seemed to suffuse her whole being. She closed the cupboard door with an angry gesture. What on earth was she doing standing there and gazing at its jumbled contents?

'Hello Caroline, how nice to find you in your old room. It

really is like coming home.'

Startled she turned and stared at him with an expression of indignation and dismay. He was alone and advanced toward her with the innocent boyish look she remembered so well. As if to fend him off she shot out an arm as rigid as a tow bar. Unperturbed he took her hand in his.

'I thought it'd be easier for both of us if I left my retinue behind,' he said lightly. He stood back and gave her an appraising look. 'You're looking very well, Caroline, and as to your work, everyone's been singing your praises since I stepped through the door this morning. I won't linger now or someone may wonder where I've got to.' He paused at the door. 'Very little seems to have changed since I left, which is reassuring. At least, I find it so.'

It was only after he had gone she realised she hadn't spoken a single word while he had been in her room.

'To think I was once in love with the bastard!' she exclaimed angrily through clenched teeth.

CHAPTER FIVE

Each year the Chief Prosecuting Solicitor and his staff held a Christmas party. Each year its hosts questioned the need to do so and thereafter faced the prospect with varying degrees of dread and irritation.

The fact that it was left to Tom Hunsey to organise did nothing to improve anyone's temper. Years back he had volunteered to undertake the unwanted chore and now, to general dismay, it had become his by prescriptive right. He never showed any inclination to relinquish it and nobody knew how to make a change. His enjoyment of the preparations became everyone else's pain and grief.

'How many white wine do you think I ought to order? . . . Only two dozen? Adrian suggested five. It is on sale or return. O.K., I'll have a word with Charles . . . And what do you think about canapés this year? They do put up the cost and last time an awful lot seemed to end up on the floor . . .'

And so it went on in the weeks preceding the party as Tom Hunsey made his remorseless rounds asking the same questions over and over again without ever listening to any answers.

Each year, too, the issue arose as to whether wives should be automatically invited and, if so, where should the additional subsidy fall. The wives themselves formed a powerful lobby and cared not who paid for them so long as they attended. So far they always had.

The guests proper included local solicitors and police officers, plus the mayor of Grainfield, a sprinkling of J.P.s from the benches before which the C.P.S.'s staff appeared and the head of the law faculty at the polytechnic who had become an established television personality.

'I'd like you to send an invitation to my in-laws, Tom,' Murray had said when Hunsey bounded into his room on his second morning to talk about arrangements for the party.

'Of course, Murray. I'll see that an invitation goes off today.'

'And Tom?'

'Yes, Murray.'

'I'd like to see the complete guest list.'

'I'll let you have one as soon as it's been typed. It should be a splendid occasion this year with you playing host for the first time and our saying a sad farewell to Edward. I'm sure it'll go with a real swing.' Abruptly he asked, 'What's your feeling about black olives?'

'I dislike them.'

'Edward has a passion for them.'

'Edward and I are two different people.'

'I think I'd better order some.'

'But of course. Edward's our guest of honour and must have all the black olives he wants.'

Hunsey let out a giggle and shook his head slowly from side to side as if enjoying a private joke. Murray frowned. Hunsey pursuing his own mysterious thoughts could be singularly irritating.

'Still waters run deep, eh, Murray?' he said suddenly with a knowing wink.

'I've no idea what you're talking about.'

'We seem such a dull lot on the surface, but who knows what goes on beneath?'

'If anyone does, I imagine it's you,' Murray observed acidly. 'But please don't try and involve me in any office

31

gossip, Tom, because I'm not interested.'

'Of course, Murray,' Hunsey said with a vague nod, as he turned and walked toward the door.

The C.P.S. watched him go with a thoughtful frown. It was only his second day, but he couldn't wait to make changes.

Once the party and Christmas were over, he would have to sharpen his axe.

CHAPTER SIX

Light snow fell on the night before the party, followed by a partial thaw. It was sufficient to make Tom Hunsey wring his hands for fear of cancellations.

'Don't worry, Tom,' Peter Shoreham said kindly. 'It takes more than a bit of slush to keep most people away from a party. Not even an earthquake would deter some I know.'

This proved to be a correct assessment and the first guests arrived punctually at six, shedding their outer garments in the relative warmth of the large and gloomy hall which was decorated with coloured paper chains and a Christmas tree whose fairy lights flickered erratically.

'Looks ghastly, doesn't it?' Peter Shoreham remarked to his wife as he helped her off with her coat. 'The decorations are five years old and the Christmas tree looks as if it's suffering from advanced mange.'

'It'll look better after a few drinks,' she said. 'Oh, there's Alison Patching. I wonder how she's enjoying retirement. Oh, you know what I mean,' she added, observing her husband's mocking eyebrow. 'And just look at Peggy Buck. Talk about Queen Victoria not being amused!'

It was true that Peggy Buck was giving the impression of someone ready to put down an imminent riot. She was standing with an imperious air waiting for her husband who was talking to George Ives.

'Hello, Caroline,' Kay Shoreham now said. 'We all seem

to have arrived together. How are you enjoying the new regime?'

Peter Shoreham groaned inwardly. He was devoted to his wife, but wished she would pay greater attention to his briefings. He had specially reminded her to be careful what she said to Caroline.

They made their way upstairs to the large conference room on the second floor in which the party was held.

Murray and Jennifer Riston stood at the door greeting everyone. He kissed Kay on the cheek and said she looked even prettier than ever. Jennifer Riston smiled and said yes, it was lovely being back in Grainfield.

Peter Shoreham hovered just inside the room to observe the imminent confrontation between Murray and Peggy Buck. He saw her take his outstretched hand without so much as a glance in his direction and sail on into the room with all the aplomb of a battle cruiser. Murray's smile remained intact and he appeared unperturbed by the snub.

'I hope that told him how I feel about his appointment,' she said as she came up to her husband.

'I doubt whether anything can penetrate a skin as thick as his,' he remarked sourly.

'I can try.' She stared about her. 'Let's go and have a word with Edward. He's looking a bit forlorn, poor man. I can see he needs rescuing.'

Edward Patching was over in a corner of the room holding a glass of white wine and making conversation with George Ives' wife. It was hard to tell which of them was under the greater strain. As Peggy Buck approached, Mrs Ives melted away with apparent relief. She detested parties and only a strong sense of duty ensured her appearance on these occasions.

'I could see you were having a sticky time with Mrs I,' Peggy said heartily. 'Nice little woman, but not exactly throbbing with party spirit. Anyway, how are you, Edward?

34

More importantly when will you and Alison come and have dinner with us?' As she spoke, she opened her handbag and pulled out a diary. 'What about Friday next week?'

'I think that's the evening we're dining with the Ristons,' Edward Patching said uneasily.

'Oh! Well, we'd better leave it until after Christmas,' she said with a sniff as she closed her handbag with the snap of a crocodile's jaws. 'I gather they're already missing you, Edward,' she went on after the briefest pause. 'Of all the disgraceful appointments. Surely you could have done something to prevent it?'

'I was never consulted,' he said coldly.

'But couldn't you have approached the committee?'

'It would have been most improper,' he replied with a touch of impatience.

'But everyone knows how much string-pulling goes on behind the scenes. Don't you realise what it's done to Charles? He believed he was in the running for appointment and then he gets this cruel slap in the face. Only mischief, if not actual malice, can have motivated them in giving the job to Murray Riston.'

'I really don't think this is the time or place for such a discussion,' Patching said uncomfortably. 'I realise Charles was disappointed and I'm sorry, but . . .'

'He's got to lump it, is that what you're telling me?'

'You're not being reasonable,' he said with a slight air of desperation holding out his glass for a refill as Tom Hunsey came bounding up with a bottle in each hand.

'The white wine's not bad, is it?' Hunsey said enthusiastically. 'Enjoying the party, Edward? Better being a guest than the host, eh?' Apart from treading on her foot, he ignored Peggy Buck as he continued to address Edward Patching. 'Going to have a word with Rex Kline?' he asked with a sly wink. 'I see he's just arrived.'

Patching frowned. 'I hope to have a word with everyone I

know,' he said loftily.

Hunsey nodded keenly. 'That's right, Edward, enjoy yourself. You're our guest of honour. We must try and have a bit of a chat later on.'

From Patching's expression a bit of a chat with Tom Hunsey was the last thing he wanted. Not that he was to avoid it. Nor for that matter did he have any burning desire to socialise with Murray Riston's father-in-law, who was, he noticed, conversing with Chief Superintendent Tarr.

'And how's Mr Kline?' Tarr enquired bluffly.

'Struggling to stay afloat,' Kline replied with a genial smile. 'It's not an easy time for us business folk. The recession's bit hard. No regular monthly pay cheques for most of us and certainly no index-linked pensions. All we can do is tighten our belts and live off fat for a while, if we're lucky enough to have any.'

Tarr gave a meaning glance at Rex Kline's well covered frame and both men laughed.

'You must be pleased about Murray's appointment,' he said.

'They couldn't have picked a better man, I'm sure of that. He was far and away the best in the field.'

'I'm afraid he may have a bit of a prickly time at first,' Tarr remarked.

'I'm sure he can deal with it.' He raised his glass. 'I drink to the committee that recognised merit and didn't just say, it's Buggins turn.'

'By which you obviously mean Charles Buck?'

'Can't stand the fellow. Officious and ill-mannered.'

'He's an effective advocate in court,' Tarr observed.

'I'm sure Murray will know how to keep him in his place,' Kline went on as if Tarr hadn't spoken.

Tarr smiled non-committally. Of one thing he was certain, Rex Kline wouldn't hesitate to try and use his son-in-law's influence if the occasion arose. There had been rumours to that effect when Murray had earlier been on the staff and was courting Jennifer, but nothing had ever been substantiated. Nevertheless, Kline was a born manipulator of people and Tarr's view of human nature was that there was nobody who was one hundred percent 'sea green incorruptible'. Not even the Pope or the Lord Chief Justice, he was wont to say.

'I must go and have a word with our host,' he said, as he observed Murray detach himself from a large blonde woman in a tight silk dress which accentuated all her contours.

As Tarr moved off, Rex Kline stared after him with a thoughtful expression, then with a shrug he turned and waylaid a passing bottle. For a while he stood observing the scene. His wife was talking to Grainfield's most prosperous solicitor and Jennifer was doing her duty with George Ives. For a few seconds all he could see were people he didn't wish to talk to, then he recognised a fellow J.P. across the room and decided to go and speak to him. He had just begun to weave his way in that direction when he was confronted by Tom Hunsey, still with a bottle in each hand.

'I don't think we've met, Mr Kline, I'm Tom Hunsey. I'm a solicitor on Murray's staff.'

Rex Kline gave him an appraising look. 'So you're Mr Hunsey? I've heard Murray mention you. I can't ever have been on the bench when you've appeared in our court.'

'We're all delighted to have Murray back,' Hunsey burbled.

'I'm glad to know that.'

'We're wondering what changes he has in store for us.'

'You'll doubtless find out when he's ready to make them.'

'So he does intend making some?'

'Now come, Mr Hunsey, you mustn't put words into my mouth. I've no idea what he has in mind. I'm not in his confidence over office matters.'

'Just wondered,' Hunsey remarked unabashed. He glanced greedy-eyed round the room. 'I expect you know quite a few people here, don't you?'

'A certain number.'

'That's Edward Patching, Murray's predecessor, over there. I think you know him all right.'

'We've met.'

'I expect he'd like to have a word with you,' Hunsey said archly, as he moved away brandishing his two bottles.

'Don't take too much notice of Tom Hunsey, Mr Kline,' Peter Shoreham said with a smile, coming up at that moment. 'I couldn't help noticing your expression.'

'Is he always like that?' Kline enquired with a frown.

'If you mean what I think you mean, the answer's yes. We're used to him here and tend to overlook his quirkiness.'

'Quirkiness you call it,' Kline remarked harshly. 'I'm not so sure . . ..' Then with a sudden change of mood he said, 'I feel I can bask in my son-in-law's glory this evening.'

'I'm sure Murray's enjoying himself, too.'

Meanwhile Hunsey was peering anxiously about him.

'Anyone seen Caroline?' he asked several people at large.

'She was here about twenty minutes ago,' someone said.

'I wonder where she is? She's coming out to dinner with me afterwards.' He sounded worried.

'She'll reappear,' the same person said. 'Anyway the party's nowhere near at an end yet.'

Hunsey was a widower who lived alone and who was wont from time to time to invite somebody home for dinner. His cooking was rudimentary and the guest was invariably required to help with the washing-up afterwards. The usual menu was soup from a tin, followed by over-grilled chops, under-cooked peas and lumpy mashed potatoes and as a final course one or two ancient pieces of cheese which had to be disentangled from their wrapping.

'I'd better go and look for her,' Hunsey said, still darting anxious looks about him.

'She may be resting,' Peggy Buck said. 'I'd leave her alone

38

if I were you, Tom.'

'Why should she be resting?'

'I don't think she was feeling awfully well. And I'm not surprised at that,' she added, casting a savage look in Murray's direction as he talked to Detective Chief Inspector Russell who was head of the Grainfield divisional C.I.D.

'I'll go and see if she's all right.'

'If you take my advice . . .'

But Peggy Buck found she was addressing a retreating back and turned crossly away.

An hour later the party had broken up. There were still one or two hardened drinkers holding out, but the general atmosphere was one of desolation with overflowing ashtrays and smeared glasses on every available surface.

'Where's Mr Riston?' a departing guest enquired of Peter Shoreham. 'I want to say goodbye to him.'

'I think he slipped out,' Peter said uncertainly. 'I expect he'll be back in a minute.'

'And has Mr Patching left?'

'I think he must have.'

'Oh dear! Will you say goodbye to Mr Riston for me and thank him for his splendid hospitality.' The guest glanced quickly about him and said in a faintly conspiratorial aside, 'I hope his appointment hasn't upset the applecart too badly.'

'I don't think I follow your meaning,' Peter remarked warily.

'I was a member of the committee that appointed him,' the man said, giving Peter a significant look. 'You don't have to pretend to me. Obviously I think we've put the right man in the right place, but I realise we've upset you know who. Incidentally where's he got to?'

'Charles Buck you mean?'

'Yes.'

'He's probably saying goodbye to somebody downstairs.'

A few minutes later Peter was standing at the top of the

stairs when George Ives came dashing into the deserted hall from outside.

'Mr Shoreham, Mr Shoreham,' he called out to Peter who was the only person in sight. 'Something terrible's happened. Mr Hunsey's dead.'

'Dead? Where?' Peter echoed stupidly.

'He's lying in the bushes halfway down the drive. There's blood all over his head. I think he's been murdered.'

CHAPTER SEVEN

It was not that Peter Shoreham doubted what George Ives had told him, but his reaction was that of somebody who was trained to check things for himself. Suddenly the place seemed to have become deserted and he was the only senior member of the staff on hand. It behoved him to find out for himself what had happened.

'Show me where you found him, George,' he said, bounding down the stairs.

Together they hurried out into the drive where the remaining snow had been churned into a brown slush. There was a one-way system whereby you entered through one pillared gateway and drove out through another about fifty yards further up the road. The area bounded by the drive and the road outside was half an acre of bushes and trees which formed one solid clump.

Ives led the way along the 'entrance' fork to where the drive made a slight kink and they were beyond any reflected light coming from the house. Suddenly he stopped and directed the beam of his torch into the bushes on their left. Peter Shoreham caught his breath as it fell on a pair of polished black shoes.

'Lend me your torch, George,' he said. 'We'd better not go trampling any closer.'

It was possible to recognise Tom Hunsey's blue pin-stripe suit. He was lying face down and his head looked as if it had burst open at the back.

'Do you mind staying here, George, and making sure nobody interferes with the scene? I'll go back to the house and get help. Fortunately departing cars go out the other way and nobody'll be arriving at this hour. I'll be as quick as I can. Incidentally, where's your wife?'

'I'd taken her home and come back. She'd got a bit tired. She's not very fond of parties.'

Peter Shoreham gave the chief clerk a sympathetic nod before turning on his heel and hurrying back along the drive.

The hall was still deserted, but voices were coming from upstairs. He was later to reflect that the picture which greeted him was similar to what happens during a stage blackout between scenes. One lot of characters melt away during the brief spell of darkness and when the lights come on again another lot have occupied the stage.

Murray Riston was in conversation with his father-in-law over in one corner and Peter wondered where they had been when he left the room not more than six or seven minutes earlier. It was with a measure of relief that he saw Detective Chief Inspector Russell and Chief Superintendent Tarr talking with Dr Sinclair, the police surgeon, on the other side of the room.

'What's happened, Peter? You look as if you've seen a whole bevy of ghosts.'

Peter turned sharply to find Charles Buck observing him from the doorway with a quizzical expression.

'It's Tom Hunsey. He's been murdered.'

Buck frowned as if he had just been informed of a minor staff misdemeanour.

'Are you being serious?' he asked suspiciously.

'His body's lying in the bushes halfway along the drive,' Peter said on a rising note of agitation.

'Then you'd better invoke the assistance of our guests over there,' Buck said, nodding in the direction of Dr Sinclair and the two police officers. 'It could also be your duty to inform the C.P.S.' It was Charles Buck's habit to indulge in strangely stilted phraseology when thrown off balance.

Peter had barely imparted his news before Tarr and Russell with Dr Sinclair, who paused to drain his glass as though it might be a last opportunity to fortify himself, hurried from the room and down the stairs.

Going over to where Murray and Rex Kline were still talking, Peter told them what had happened.

'Murdered?' Murray said disbelievingly.

'I'm afraid so.'

'Who on earth would want to murder Tom Hunsey?' Giving Peter a wry smile he added, 'Silly question! I suppose I'd better wait here until the experts return.' He glanced round the room. 'Everyone else seems to have disappeared anyway. Where's Charles Buck? I saw him talking to you a moment ago.'

'He may have followed the others outside.'

'All the more reason, then, for me to stay put. Let's go and sit down and you can tell me a few more details.'

By the time Peter had completed his brief recital of events, Murray was looking curiously irresolute, while Rex Kline, who had wandered off and recharged his glass, was standing nearby glowering at nothing in particular.

'I think I'll go and find out what's happening,' Peter said in an effort to ease the atmosphere.

As he reached the top of the stairs, he met his wife and Jennifer Riston.

'We've been having a girls talk in the so-called ladies powder room,' Kay said. 'I do think someone might have removed the rack of smelly pipes for the occasion.' She paused and peered more closely at her husband. 'You've got a funny look, Peter. Has anything happened?'

'I'm afraid Tom Hunsey's dead. He's been killed. The police are already investigating. Why don't you go and wait in my room? I'll be back as soon as I can.'

'Where's Murray?' Jennifer asked in an anxious tone.

'He's in there with your father.'

'I must go to him,' Jennifer said, darting away.

'I'll wait there, too,' Kay said in a subdued tone.

As Peter turned to go downstairs, he heard a door close with a soft click. He was almost sure it was Caroline's. It didn't strike him, however, as being of any significance.

He was about to go out of the front door when he chanced to look at the desk used by Alec, the doorkeeper. It had been pushed back against the wall to give greater space and its surface was clear of objects. Obviously Alec had put away in a drawer the visitors' book and his assortment of coloured ballpoint pens, also the lethal ebony ruler he had been presented with by a friendly police officer after a madman had run amok one day some years before and attacked him with a penknife. It resembled an ordinary ruler, but it had been hollowed out and filled with lead to make it a particularly vicious cosh. Indeed it had been used as such by the criminal from whom it had been seized in the course of the robbery. Alec had been delighted with the gift and frequently sat caressing it when he wasn't attending to other business.

By the time Peter reached the scene a police car had been manoeuvred into a position where its headlights shone into the bushes. Tarr and Russell were crouched over the body.

Charles Buck was talking to Dr Sinclair beside the car. The doctor turned as Peter came up.

'Looks as if the poor chap received a violent karate chop across the front of his throat and was then beaten about the head with a heavy instrument of some sort.' He gave Peter a sombre look. 'What an end to a Christmas party! With luck they'll find the weapon somewhere in the bushes. Tarr's already sent for reinforcements.' Grimly he added, 'With senior police officers amongst your guests and their

44

headquarters up the road, no murder enquiry can have got off to a better start. And that means a far better chance of catching the murderer.'

Peter glanced at Charles Buck who was standing silently thoughtful. He looked up and met Peter's gaze. In a mocking tone he said, 'Let's hope our new C.P.S. has a good alibi.'

CHAPTER EIGHT

As Tarr was to remark later, it was surprising how many people came out of the woodwork. He was referring to the number of guests who suddenly reappeared as the news spread. Leaving Detective Chief Inspector Russell at the scene, he had returned to the house with two newly arrived officers to begin preliminary enquiries. First he called for a complete list of guests with their addresses, then he made a roll call of those still present. One of the officers was despatched to record the registration numbers of every car within the precincts, a move which Peter Shoreham saw as being extremely astute.

While those still on the premises were being coralled in the conference room, Peter slipped away to see if he could find Caroline whose prolonged absence had begun to worry him. He was aware that she had been going out to dinner with Tom Hunsey that evening and it seemed more than likely that she was somewhere in the building. Besides which he was still sure it had been her door that had been closed with a gentle click as he stood at the top of the stairs.

He reached the end of the corridor and knocked on it. A faint sound came from within. Opening the door a fraction, he said softly. 'It's me, Peter, Caroline. May I come in?'

'Yes, come in,' she said in a voice that clearly told him she had been crying.

The room was in darkness, but, as he entered, she

switched on her desk lamp, quickly adjusting the shade so that her face remained in shadow.

'Are you all right?' he asked anxiously.

'I couldn't stick it in there any longer,' she said with a catch in her voice. 'I thought I'd be all right, but suddenly everything got too much and I just wanted to be alone. And I have a splitting headache.'

'Have you been in your room all the time?'

'Mmm! I wanted to go home, but I'd promised to have dinner with Tom.'

'Hasn't Tom come looking for you?' he asked in a puzzled tone.

'Nobody's come looking for me, thank goodness! I'd have locked my door, but I've lost the key.'

'And you've been here all the time?'

'Yes. I told you so just now.'

'Tom was asking everyone if they'd seen you. I assumed he would have looked for you here.'

She shook her head in a vague manner. After a short silence she said in a tone whose bleakness chilled him, 'I didn't believe Murray's return would disturb my peace of mind the way it has. I'll have to go or I'll have a breakdown.'

She buried her face abruptly in her hands and began to cry.

Peter went over to the desk and put a comforting arm round her shoulder.

'We all know what a strain you've been under, but you've got to bear up. Something's happened. Something terrible. Tom's been murdered.'

'Murdered? Tom Hunsey? Well, there's only one person who could have done that, isn't there?' she burst out, staring up at him with a wild look.

Peter clapped a hand over her mouth. 'Don't talk like that!' he said fiercely. 'Just think what you're going to say to the police about your own movements. They'll want to see

47

you before you go home. Incidentally, Kay and I will take you back. You can leave your car here overnight.' He paused and gazed down at her. She had a normally strong face, but at this moment it was distorted with fear and worry. 'Would you like me to fetch you a brandy? It'll help steady your nerves.'

'What are you going to tell the police? About me, I mean?'

'If they ask me, I shall say I found you in your room and that you told me you'd left the party because you had a bad headache.'

'I'm sorry I became a bit emotional, Peter,' she said, giving him a wan look.

'It was understandable. You had every cause to be.'

But was it, he wondered? It seemed inconceivable that Tom Hunsey had not sought her in her room and yet she said she had been there all the time and nobody had entered. Moreover he was still sure it was her door he had heard being closed, though that didn't necessarily mean she had been out of her room. Nevertheless, it was puzzling.

He had known Caroline for eight years and was fond of her. They had always enjoyed a comfortable brother sister relationship. If he could protect her he would.

CHAPTER NINE

Although the investigation of a murder was a matter for the C.I.D., Tarr had no hesitation in assuming virtual command of the enquiry. He reckoned he knew the C.P.S.'s staff better than any of his colleagues and since his promotion and transfer to the uniform branch he had not been able to keep his nose out of any C.I.D. case that particularly interested him. In the present instance he supposed he could even be briefly classified as a suspect. At all events he had no intention of stepping aside and leaving Detective Chief Inspector Russell to get on with things, even though he was in nominal charge of enquiries.

'I think I'll go and see Mr Patching, Stephen,' he said to Russell about an hour after the discovery of Hunsey's body. 'I assume he'll be at home.'

'O.K., sir,' Russell said gloomily. Indeed there was little else he could say, but that didn't make things any better. Not for the first time he wished he was attached to a division in which the Chief Superintendent in charge left his C.I.D. officers to their own devices.

Though Tarr had known Edward Patching for upwards of fifteen years and had met him on many social occasions, he had only once visited him at his home and that had been before his divorce when he and his first wife occupied a small but charming Tudor house within the precincts of Grainfield Abbey. Tarr knew he had been forced to sell this in order to pay for the divorce settlement, but hadn't realised how far down the scale of 'desirable residences' he had sunk until he turned his car into the new housing estate where the Patchings now lived. Even in the dark, he was able to appreciate what a comedown it had been.

He recognised Patching's car parked outside and saw light coming from the curtained front window.

He pressed the doorbell which made a noise like a buzzsaw. A few moments later a porch light was switched on and Alison Patching opened the door.

'Oh, it's you, Mr Tarr. I expect you want to see Edward. He's been terribly shocked by the news. What an awful thing to have happened!' She spoke breathlessly as if she had just run up and down stairs several times.

'You've heard, then?'

'Yes, Charles Buck phoned about an hour ago. Come in, Edward's in the living room. I've just persuaded him to have a sip of brandy. He found the party something of a strain anyway and then this news on top of it . . .'

She led the way into a room off the hall. It was warm and lit by two standard lamps, one each side of the fireplace where a modern gas fire glowed agreeably. It was the sort of room that appeared nightly in telly ads for soothing bedtime drinks.

Edward Patching was sitting in an armchair staring at the fire. He turned his head as Tarr came in.

'I can scarcely believe it,' he said painfully. 'Is it really true?'

'I'm afraid so.'

'When did it happen?'

'His body was found by George Ives around eight-twenty. Ives dashed back to the house and told Peter Shoreham, who was the first person he saw. Shoreham accompanied him back to the scene before informing myself and Chief Inspector Russell. Fortunately we were still there.' He paused. 'How much did Mr Buck tell you on the phone?'

'Simply that Tom Hunsey had been found battered to death in the bushes down the drive and that a full-scale murder enquiry was under way.' He gave a shiver. 'I still can't believe it.'

'When did you last see Hunsey yourself?'

Edward Patching pursed his lips. 'It couldn't have been long before I left,' he said wearily. 'He was going round filling up people's glasses and breaking into conversations in the tiresome way he used to. I had the impression he'd had a bit too much to drink himself. As you probably know he organised the party every year and liked to believe he was responsible for its success. Nobody ever had the heart to tell him it'd be much easier if he bowed out and left it to others to run. Poor chap! One mustn't speak ill of the dead, but he had become something of a trial to all of us.'

'You're not telling me anything I don't know,' Tarr remarked. 'There isn't an officer in my division who didn't dread having him assigned to one of their cases.'

'I know. And yet he was so good in his younger days. But he seemed to lose his ability to make up his mind. He degenerated into a ditherer.'

'And a gossipmonger from what I've heard.'

'I know he had that reputation,' Patching said with a sorrowful nod.

'Can you think of anyone who had a possible motive for killing him?'

'Absolutely not! I hope you're not suggesting he was killed by a colleague?'

'It must be a possibility.'

'I refuse to accept it,' Patching said disdainfully.

'I'd even put it as a probability,' Tarr went on unperturbed. 'If it wasn't a colleague, it was obviously somebody at the party. Somebody who knew him.'

'Why do you say that?' Patching asked in a suddenly

51

anguished tone.

'Because I simply don't believe it was a casual intruder he surprised in the bushes. It doesn't make sense. What would an intruder have been doing in your drive on a cold December night?'

'He might have been looking for a car to take.'

'Extremely unlikely,' Tarr said dismissively. 'In my view, it was somebody who knew him and who had a sudden burning motive to kill him.'

'Why do you say sudden?'

'Because my supposition is that the murderer followed him outside and killed him as soon as they were away from the house. If I'm right, it was a murder of sudden necessity, otherwise a better time and place would have been chosen. It was premeditated all right, but not over a long period.'

Edward Patching gave a resigned shrug. 'I still can't believe he was murdered by a colleague. It's bad enough he's been killed, without that possibility. I feel stunned and sickened. I'd known him all the time I've been C.P.S. and whatever his faults, he didn't deserve such a terrible fate.'

'I take it Mr Buck told you how he'd been killed?' Tarr said after a pause.

'Yes, battered to death, as I mentioned earlier. Have you found the weapon?'

'Not yet, but I'm sure we shall quite soon. It's probably somewhere in the bushes. The odds are the murderer threw it away immediately.'

The telephone rang out in the hall and Alison Patching, who had been in the kitchen, answered it.

'It's Detective Chief Inspector Russell, Mr Tarr,' she said, poking her head round the door.

'Thought I'd let you know, sir, that we've found the weapon,' Russell said as soon as Tarr came on the line. 'It was an eighteen inch ruler, a round ebony one . . .'

'Filled with lead,' Tarr broke in.

'That's right, sir. I take it you also know where it came from?'

'From the doorkeeper's desk. It was given him several years ago by Sergeant Hunter after he'd been assaulted by some nut case. Where did you find it?'

'In the bushes about twenty yards from the body. The murderer obviously hurled it away afterwards.'

'What I'd have expected. With luck, it'll have some fingerprints.'

'With luck,' Russell said in a none too hopeful tone. 'Has Mr Patching been able to throw any light on what's happened?'

'None so far. He appears considerably shocked by the news, but that's understandable.'

In Tarr's view, the retired C.P.S. was a weak but stubborn man who vacillated in a crisis.

'How's the interviewing going at your end, Stephen?' he now asked.

'Terrible. It's like questioning witnesses in an affray case. Everybody's seen something, but none of it seems to fit together. It appears that Hunsey went off looking for Miss Allard and for some reason his search took him outside, though I've not yet found anyone who actually saw him leave the house. He was last seen at the top of the stairs holding a bottle of wine in each hand. He obviously took them with him because we've found two bottles a few feet from the body. They were hidden in long grass which is why we didn't spot them in the first instance.'

'Do you mean deliberately hidden?'

'No, no. It looks as if he flung out his arms and dropped them when he was attacked. Heaven knows why he took them out of the house with him.'

'If you'd known him as well as I did, you'd understand. He'd have been capable of walking home with them. He once came back into court to pick up a law report he'd left there carrying a stuffed otter under his arm that he'd just bought in the shop next door. He was quite oblivious of the astonishment and near hysteria he caused.'

'I knew he was a bit of an oddball, but not that short of his marbles.' He paused. 'Do you agree, sir, that everything points to it being an inside job? I mean, that the murderer was known to his victim?'

'That's how it looks to me. I don't think I'm going to find out much more here, so I'll come back to the Manor.'

Edward Patching was still sitting staring into the fire when Tarr returned to the room.

'They've found the weapon,' he said. 'It was that loaded ruler Alec kept on his desk.' Patching closed his eyes and his face assumed an expression of horror. He didn't say anything, however, and Tarr went on, 'Which supports my belief that the murderer must have followed Hunsey out of the house.' He stared at Patching with a touch of impatience. 'Sooner or later you'll have to face up to the fact that murderer and victim were probably drinking together earlier in the evening.'

'It's worse than any nightmare I've ever had,' Patching murmured in a desolate tone.

Tarr shrugged. One didn't expect a man of sixty-two, who had spent most of his life serving the law in its seamier and more violent contexts, to react like someone who has never been in contact with sudden death.

'I'm sorry I can't help you more, Mr Tarr,' he said in the same effortful voice. 'I'll try and pull myself together and write you out a statement. I ought to know by now the sort of details you want. What contact I had with Tom Hunsey at the party, when I last saw him, what time I left and whether I noticed anything untoward about him. As you realise from what I've told you, it'll be a somewhat negative statement, but I'll put it all down on paper and let you have it tomorrow.'

'The sooner, the better.' Tarr seemed about to get up, but then sat back in his chair again. 'Before I go, I'd like you to think very carefully whether you mayn't be able to help me over motive. I won't ask you to speculate in your written statement, but I should like you to do some thinking aloud for my private ear. One of your late staff has been brutally done to death and you owe it to him to see that his killer is brought to trial. It's not a time for closed ranks and so-called loyalty to ex-colleagues. It's your duty to tell the police every nuance of gossip you possess that might throw light on what's happened. You can trust us to act discreetly.'

'Of course, of course! Nobody has greater respect for the police than I, but it's not fair . . .' His voice trailed away.

'What's not fair?' Tarr asked with the determination of a boxer landing a punch.

'To tell you anything I can't support with evidence.'

'Look, Mr Patching, we're not dissecting a case in your office and assessing its merits. All I'm trying to do is pick up a scent and, as you well know, motive is usually the strongest scent in a murder enquiry.' He fixed the retired C.P.S. with a hard stare. 'I need you to tell me who you think may have committed this crime.'

Edward Patching shook his head helplessly. 'As C.P.S. I was above any gossip that went on in the office. I had no wish to become involved in matters that weren't my official concern. I made a point of turning a deaf ear to any tittle-tattle.'

'We're not talking about tittle-tattle, we're discussing motives for murder. The odds are that somebody known to you murdered Hunsey and I'm sure you can provide me with a line of enquiry. I give you my word that I won't publicly divulge anything you tell me. It's your duty to help me, though I shouldn't need to tell you that. I'm asking you to confide your suspicions in me.'

Patching nibbled nervously at the back of one of his

fingers.

'You're making things very difficult for me, Mr Tarr.' He shifted uneasily in his chair. 'It goes back several years and concerned Mr Riston when he was previously on the staff. There was a suggestion that he and a certain police officer connived to protect Rex Kline from criminal proceedings in respect of a business transaction that caused him to sail closer to the wind than was prudent. There were rumours that Kline might have obtained money by deception, but that the police officer in question was bribed to, how shall I put it, look the other way.'

'And that Mr Riston acted as intermediary?'

'Yes.'

'You're forgetting that I was a D.I. at the time and knew all about the enquiry. There was never any evidence to support a charge in respect of the allegation of obtaining money by deception, nor any evidence that he tried to bribe the officer in question. Indeed, I recall quite clearly that it was a thoroughly scurrilous rumour that had been put about by a business rival with whom he'd recently quarrelled.'

'I'm afraid I was forgetting you knew the details,' Patching said coldly.

Tarr brushed aside the apology if such it was and said, 'What I'd like to know is how you relate that incident to Hunsey's murder?'

'I'm not seeking to make any connection. I was only trying to offer you a possible line of enquiry. You may be satisfied that there was nothing to the rumour, Mr Tarr, but not everyone necessarily shares your belief.'

'Who, for example?' Tarr asked.

'Mr Buck, for one.'

'I realise he has good cause to resent Murray Riston's appointment as C.P.S., but I don't see where Hunsey fits in.'

'Tom Hunsey may have found out something which suggested that Mr Riston did go beyond the bounds of propriety and did cover up for his future father-in-law.'

'What could Hunsey have discovered that the police failed to uncover?' Tarr asked sharply.

'I'm merely speculating at *your* invitation. You'll recall that I expressed a strong desire not to be drawn into this sort of exercise. Tom Hunsey had a strong propensity for digging out scandal. He was, indeed, a pastmaster at it.'

'But I thought you refused to listen to staff gossip.'

'I did, but sometimes Hunsey would say something before you could stop him.'

'And he told you he suspected Mr Riston of improper conduct when he was here before?'

'He hinted at it, but I told him I didn't want to hear.'

'When was that?' Tarr asked drily.

'Just after Mr Riston's appointment had been announced.'

'As recently as that?' Tarr said in a surprised tone. 'What would have been his source of information?'

'I've no idea,' Patching said with a disdainful shrug.

'Doesn't it probably mean there's something hidden away in your office files?'

'I doubt if you'd find anything incriminating there. One would expect such evidence, if it ever existed, to have been removed.'

'I suppose so. On the other hand, we may have to check through some of them if we're really stuck.' He paused. 'So what you're saying to me in effect is, keep an eye on the new C.P.S., check his alibi and dig deeper for his motive.'

Two small spots of colour appeared on Patching's cheeks.

'I've said no such thing,' he said indignantly.

'No?'

'I trust I haven't sunk to that sordid level.'

'All crime is sordid,' Tarr remarked impatiently. 'Anyway, apart from Mr Riston, can you think of anyone else who might have wanted Hunsey out of the way?'

'Certainly not.'

'Though from what you've told me, as well as from my own knowledge of him, he was obviously somebody who lived for gossip and thrived on scandal.'

'I'm afraid so.'

'Those sort of people can seldom resist the temptation of hinting how clever they are.' Tarr became thoughtful for a moment before adding, 'Show off your cleverness to the wrong person and you may be signing your own death warrant.'

CHAPTER TEN

On returning to Grainfield Manor Tarr parked behind two police cars on the grass verge outside the entrance and then walked up the exit side of the drive. Arc lights shone from within the bushes on his left, giving the impression of a scene being shot for television.

As he stepped inside the hall, Chief Inspector Russell came out of a door on his left and made for the staircase. Catching sight of Tarr, he stopped and gave him a wary smile.

'I've got people being interviewed in every ruddy room,' he remarked. 'Quite a number of guests have come back voluntarily as the news spread. I reckon their motives were more ghoulish than a desire to help, but I mustn't grumble. It's saved us traipsing over the countryside trying to locate them.'

'Any of them got anything to offer?'

'Not so far. It's like I said on the phone. It'll be a question of checking and cross-checking every statement, re-interviewing people and still probably getting nowhere. Not until we discover a motive, that is.'

'That's what we have to concentrate on. Motive.'

Tarr related what Patching had said and Russell frowned.

'I've spoken to Mr Riston myself and he never left the floor where the party was held the whole evening.'

'Is that what he says?'

'Yes. Even so, I doubt whether he could have got away for long without his absence being noticed. After all, he was the host.'

'It needn't have taken more than a few minutes to have followed Hunsey down the drive and clubbed him to death. And don't forget people become less conscious of time as a party progresses. You think only five minutes have passed if you're talking to a pretty girl and find it nearer twenty. So I wouldn't discount the possibility of Riston having managed to slip away without being noticed. Nevertheless, I don't think he did it – not a clumsy murder such as this.'

'You think he would have planned it better?' Russell enquired wryly.

'Yes. That's precisely what I think.'

'But events may have forced his hand. The murderer may have had to act on the spur of the moment.'

'I agree it looks like that,' Tarr observed thoughtfully and went on, 'I wonder what happened to make Hunsey's death so immediately imperative? There was the buffoon wandering around filling people's glasses and plugging in on their conversations and the next thing is he's been beaten to death in the bushes down the drive, where he'd apparently gone looking for Miss Allard. I take it you've spoken to her? What does she have to say about it?'

'Detective Inspector Bonham's interviewing her now. I gather she left the party because of a headache and went to her room to rest.'

Tarr pulled a face. 'May or may not be significant. We'll soon know.'

The two officers turned their heads at the sound of footsteps on the stairs.

'Do you mind if I drive my wife home?' Murray Riston asked. 'I'll come back immediately.'

'That'll be all right,' Tarr said with a nod.

'Really there's no need, darling,' Jennifer said. 'I'm sure

daddy would take me.'

'My father-in-law feels he should stay as long as you may wish to interview him,' Murray said. 'Not that he has anything useful to say.'

'I'm sorry to keep him hanging about,' Russell said. 'I'll try and find a free officer who can interview Mr Kline now.'

'I think he's quite happy,' Murray said with a slight grin. 'He's just found a bottle of scotch hidden away.' In a more sombre tone he added, 'What a nightmare it's turned out to be! I'd never have come back to Grainfield if I'd known what was in store. Come on, Jennifer, I'll drive you home.'

The two officers were half way up the stairs when they were confronted by Detective Inspector Bonham.

'I've just been interviewing Miss Allard, sir,' he said in his somewhat portentous tone. 'I noticed she had fresh scratch marks on the back of her right hand. The sort you get from thrusting your way through bushes.'

'Did you ask her about them?' Russell said.

Bonham nodded. 'She pretended to be surprised, as if she'd not noticed them before. She said she must have got them tending the plants in her room. As a matter of fact, sir, you can hardly see out of her window for pots of green foliage.'

'It sounds an unlikely story,' Russell observed.

'I think you ought to question her, sir,' Bonham said. 'In my view a doctor should be asked to examine the scratches and give an opinion.'

But when Russell went looking for her, it was to find she had just been taken home by the Shorehams. Must have gone down a back staircase, he reflected. Ruddy rabbit warren of a house.

CHAPTER ELEVEN

Caroline rejected Kay Shoreham's suggestion that she should stop the night with them. She even declined their invitation to come in for a nightcap.

'It's sweet of you, but I'll be all right,' she said with great insistence. 'I'm used to being on my own. I assure you I'm not going to dissolve into hysterics.'

'I'm sure you're not; even so . . .' Kay glanced at her husband for support.

'Caroline knows we're on the end of a phone if she wants us,' Peter said in his usual practical fashion.

In the event, therefore, they dropped her at the cottage about three miles from Grainfield Manor where she had lived for the past four years.

'What time shall I pick you up in the morning?' Peter asked, as she got out of the car. 'I'm in court, but I shall have to go to the office first. What about you?'

'I've got some officers coming in at ten for a conference.'

'Then I'll call for you about nine.'

'I could really have driven myself home quite well and then there wouldn't have been all this trouble,' she said in a tone that was almost resentful.

'I hope she is all right,' Kay said doubtfully as she and her husband drove away. 'She didn't sound it just now.'

'She's upset and which of us isn't? She'll be all right. She has a good robust spirit.'

'But you're worried about her, aren't you, Peter? I can tell.' She cast an anxious glance at her husband's face.

'I'm sure she didn't murder Tom Hunsey if that's what you mean,' he said, giving her a quick smile.

Kay lapsed into silence. She knew that something was troubling him about Caroline and that sooner or later he would tell her. Meanwhile she knew him well enough to realise there was no point in pressing him further now.

As soon as she got indoors, Caroline went into her sitting-room and turned on further lights. She had drawn the curtains before leaving for the party and always made a practice of putting on at least two downstairs lights when going out in the evening. Though she didn't live on the fashionable and well burglarised side of Grainfield, her cottage was relatively isolated and was therefore a tempting target for the burglar who only went after cash. Moreover she possessed a number of items of sentimental value that had belonged to her grandmother.

Settling herself into a chair beside the telephone, she dialled a London number and let out a sigh of relief when a familiar voice answered.

'Hello, Rosa, it's Caroline.'

Though Caroline was six years older than Rosa Epton they had sat next to one another at law college where they had occupied the back row of the class, presenting a slightly incongruous picture, the elfin-like Rosa and the infinitely more substantial Caroline. They had taken their solicitors' finals at the same time and remained friends ever since. Once to their intellectual enjoyment they had met in court when Rosa came down to Grainfield to defend someone on a motoring charge and Caroline was the prosecutor. Rosa's client had been acquitted but was refused costs which, they felt, left them more or less even. For as long as Caroline had been on the staff of the Prosecuting Solicitor, Rosa had been in private practice and was now a partner in the west London firm of Snaith and Epton.

'I won't beat about the bush, Rosa, but I think I may be in trouble. No, not that sort of trouble,' she added quickly as she could see Rosa jumping to a wrong conclusion. 'We had our office Christmas party this evening and someone was murdered. Tom Hunsey. I'm sure I've mentioned him to you. He was found dead with head injuries in the bushes down the drive.' She paused and blurted out, 'The awful thing is that I was meant to be having dinner with him after the party.'

'What a terrible thing to have happened,' Rosa said in a sympathetic voice. 'But why may you be in trouble, Caroline?'

'It's . . . it's difficult to talk about on the phone.'

'Would you like me to drive down?'

'Would you, Rosa?' Caroline said in a tone of heartfelt relief.

'Of course. I was taking tomorrow off anyway. If I set out in the next half hour, I should be with you around one o'clock.'

'I'll probably keep you up the rest of the night. Trouble is I have a con with police at ten tomorrow morning and I daren't change it or people will start putting two and two together and making heaven knows what number.'

'Well, stop worrying and wait till I arrive.' After a slight pause, Rosa added, 'I might be talking to a client from the sound of me.'

'You probably are,' Caroline said bleakly.

Rosa lived in a small flat at the top of a house on Campden Hill in Kensington which put her on the right side of London for getting down to Grainfield. It was a few minutes after eleven o'clock when she locked her front door and set off down the fifty-eight stairs to the pavement where her car was parked.

64

Though she and Caroline often went months without seeing each other, they never experienced any difficulty picking up the threads. In between times they would talk on the telephone. Each found it useful to have a friend on the other side of the professional fence in a completely different area of operation from her own.

Once a year Caroline would come up to town for a weekend and they would go to the theatre and eat out and relax in one another's company for a few hours. These visits would take place in the winter and be followed by a summer visit to Grainfield by Rosa when most of the time would, weather permitting, be spent in the garden.

They were two self-contained professional women with a number of common interests who enjoyed an easy, uncomplicated friendship.

As Rosa handled purely criminal work it had never entered her head that Caroline might ever need her services. But now as she drove westwards she recalled her parting words on the phone. Caroline couldn't really be in any serious trouble. Surely not. And yet she had jumped at Rosa's offer to drive eighty miles through the night and one didn't usually let a friend do that without cogent reason.

The nearer she came to Grainfield, the more sombre became her thoughts. Fortunately the dangerous road conditions absorbed much of her concentration and kept her mind off what lay ahead.

It was nearly one thirty before she pulled up outside Caroline's cottage. Almost immediately the front door opened and Caroline stood there silhouetted against the light.

'What a friend!' she said with a half-sob as she embraced Rosa. 'Come and sit by the fire while I scramble you some eggs and make tea. Or would you sooner have something different?'

'Just the tea without the scrambled eggs. I don't need

anything to eat.'

'I'm sure you ought to eat something. It won't take a minute to scramble eggs.'

'But I had scrambled eggs for supper not long before I set out,' Rosa said with a smile.

'Soup then?'

'No, just tea. And I'll watch you boil the kettle.'

She followed Caroline out to the kitchen and perched herself on the edge of the table.

'It seems a thousand years ago,' Caroline said in a desolate tone. 'The party, I mean. I still can't believe it happened. Tom's murder, I mean.' She paused and shook her head as if in a daze. 'And to think I could have behaved so stupidly.' She gave Rosa a sudden fierce stare. 'So unbelievably stupidly . . .'

'I'll carry the tray,' Rosa broke in, seizing it from Caroline's unsteady grasp. A few minutes later when they were sitting down and the tea had been poured, she went on, 'I'm ready to listen when you're ready to talk.'

'I've lied to the police, Rosa,' Caroline said bleakly. 'Lied to them in one of those moments of . . . of . . . not so much panic as out of fear of becoming involved. They're not the same thing, you know.' After a pause in which she seemed to find difficulty in expressing her thoughts, she went on, 'They asked me if I'd been in my room all the time after slipping away from the party and I said I had.'

'But you hadn't?' Rosa said in a coaxing tone.

Caroline nodded. 'No, I hadn't.' She paused again and smiled wanly. 'Here you are waiting to hear a well ordered account and all you're getting is a disconnected story that's started in the middle anyway.'

'At some stage of the party you retired to your office?' Rosa said in an attempt at encouragement.

Caroline nodded. 'I couldn't bear it there a moment longer. I'd got a splitting headache and I was due to go out to dinner afterwards with Tom Hunsey, which was the last thing I wanted to do.' She began to weep quietly. 'It's a horrid thing to say in the circumstances, but I have to be in the right mood to take his company and I certainly wasn't tonight. I should never have accepted, but he asked me such ages ago and . . . well, you know how it is, Rosa?' Rosa nodded sympathetically and after a further pause Caroline went on, 'I guessed he'd come looking for me and so I sat in the dark in my room for a long time. But knowing Tom I realised he'd come barging in, turning on lights and calling out my name. I did think of hiding behind my filing cabinet. Then the indignity of being discovered crouching there went through my mind and I decided to creep out. Also I thought some fresh air might help my headache. So I tiptoed down a back staircase. But as I was slipping out of the front door, he spotted me and came after me. I hurried down the drive with but one thought in my head, to hide from him. I didn't want to have to try and explain what I was doing. What could I have said anyway? I heard him call out my name and I realised he'd probably catch me up, so I shot into the bushes beside the drive, thinking I'd wait there until he gave up and returned to the house. I plunged in quite a way when I suddenly heard a terrible sound behind me. It was a sort of gasp and gurgle and was followed by several dull thuds. I looked round but couldn't see anything as the bushes had closed behind me. Then I heard laboured breathing, as if somebody was out of breath. Soon after that there were further sounds of movement in the bushes, followed by complete silence. I was petrified and just stood motionless for a minute or two. Then I pushed on through the undergrowth and came out on the other arm of the drive. I managed to get back to my room without being seen and set about repairing the damage. Luckily I always keep a spare pair of outdoor shoes in my room and had put them on before going out, so my party shoes were still clean and dry. My dress hadn't suffered as much as it might have and I was able to brush off the few spots of dirt. Then I just sat and awaited events. I knew that sooner or later somebody would come looking for me. I half knew that something awful had happened and that I was responsible. Eventually Peter Shoreham came to my room – you remember meeting him, Rosa? – and he told me that Tom Hunsey had been found murdered. He asked me if I'd been there the whole time and I said I had. I told him that the combination of drink and being in the same room as Murray Riston had thrown me into an emotional turmoil and that I'd had to get away.' She gave Rosa a miserable look. 'Whatever happens, I can't stay on the staff here. Anyway, later when the police interviewed me I told them the same as I'd told Peter, namely that I'd not left my room. The officer asked me about these scratches on the back of my hand and I said I must have got them from one of the plants on my window sill.'

'Did he appear to accept that explanation?'

'He didn't make any comment, but he obviously stored it away. Stored it away with the other lie I'd told him.' She began to weep again. 'I feel I lured Tom to his death,' she said between painful sobs.

'Do you have any idea who might have killed him?' Rosa asked.

'No, I never saw anyone at all. I just heard those dreadful sounds in the bushes when he was obviously being killed. Somebody must have followed him while he was following me.' She gave a convulsive shudder. 'What on earth made me tell those lies, Rosa?' she asked in an anguished voice.

'Let me see the scratches on your hand,' Rosa said.

Caroline held out her right hand and Rosa could see two linear scratches on the back where the skin had been abraded. There was no sign of actual bleeding.

'Have you put something on them?'

'Yes, but the officer'll still remember them, just as he'll

remember my stupid lie about their cause.'

Rosa fell silently thoughtful, aware that Caroline was observing her as if awaiting some oracular pronouncement.

'At best,' she said at length, 'the police will make an earlier arrest and you won't even be drawn into the case. They'll forget about the scratches. For all we know they may already have charged someone with Tom Hunsey's murder.'

'And at worst?' Caroline said grimly.

'At worst, they'll question you further.'

'What you're saying is, they'll suspect me. They'll prove I lied to them and they'll want to know why.'

'Where are the outdoor shoes you wore?'

'In a cupboard in my office, waiting to tell their own story and bear proof of yet a further lie.'

'In what way?'

'They're sopping wet and though I gave them a quick rub over, I'm sure somebody could find tell-tale marks on them.'

'Can anyone prove a motive against you?'

'God knows we all felt like murdering Tom Hunsey at one time or another. He could be utterly infuriating. And yet he had a soft streak in him. I remember how distressed he was when some unfortunate cyclist was killed one night by a hit and run motorist not far from where Tom lived. He couldn't stop talking about it for weeks afterwards. He happened to be first on the scene and it affected him deeply.'

'When was that?'

'A few years ago. Not long after Murray left to go up north.' Caroline paused and went on in a reflective tone, 'Tom was an odd mixture of kindness, obtuseness and mischief-making. I could never make up my mind whether, at times, he was deliberately malicious or not.'

'Somebody obviously had a strong motive for murdering him,' Rosa observed.

It was Caroline who broke the silence that followed.

'I said on the phone, Rosa, that you might find you had a

client. If the worst comes to the worst, will you represent me?'

'Of course I will, but mightn't you do better to go to one of your local solicitors?'

Caroline shook her head vigorously. 'I'd be very grateful if you could stay down here tomorrow – I suppose I mean today – and see what happens. I'd like you to be present if the police want to interview me again.'

'Won't that look suspicious? I mean, innocent people, particularly solicitors on the staff of the local C.P.S., don't dash for a lawyer at the drop of a pin.'

'The Grainfield police under Chief Superintendent Tarr are as unsentimental a bunch of highwaymen as you're likely to meet,' Caroline said with considerable bitterness. 'They'd even enjoy arresting their own grandmothers.'

CHAPTER TWELVE

It had been after three when Caroline and Rosa eventually went to bed. But as so often happened after a late night, Rosa awoke early. It was still dark outside and she switched on the bedside lamp and reached for her watch, which showed the time as half past six. Leaving the light on she lay back and addressed her mind to what had happened the previous evening. Unless the police had a definite lead, it was certain they would question Caroline further. Indeed, if they had found her wet shoes in the cupboard, they might think they already had a lead.

Rosa knew of Caroline's involvement with Murray Riston and how it had thrown her when he had terminated their relationship. Rosa had met him a couple of times when he and Caroline were going out together and had never been able to make up her mind about him. Though he had been charming and friendly toward her, she had had doubts about his integrity. These, however, she had kept to herself even after his break-up with Caroline.

She now reached the conclusion that though Caroline always gave the impression of being one of those immensely sane and practical people, she was, like many others, capable of erratic behaviour on the rare occasion.

Rosa could see what a traumatic experience it had been with Tom Hunsey being killed within a few yards of where she was standing, but she wouldn't have expected her to have lied to the police in the way she had. Rosa could only think she really had been in a highly emotional state at the time. Caroline had said as much and had given it as her reason for creeping away from the party and taking refuge in her room.

Rosa hoped she would not be called upon to act as Caroline's legal adviser. It was certainly not a role she sought. Moreover, she was far from convinced that it was a good idea. Representing personal friends always presented hazards and for one female solicitor to represent another, who was also a friend, struck her as bizarre, though she wasn't quite sure whether this was a fair reaction. Maybe it was only the novelty of it that required getting used to.

It didn't enter her mind, even as a slender possibility, that Caroline could have committed the murder. She supposed the police might suspect her, but suspicion was not evidence and it was inconceivable that she could be charged. What she might have to face was a further interrogation in which she would either have to stick by the lies she had told or explain them away as plausibly as possible.

It was while she was pondering these two courses of action that she heard Caroline go downstairs. About ten minutes later there was a knock on her door and Caroline came in with a cup of tea.

'I saw your light was on so I knew you must be awake,' she said. 'Did you sleep at all?'

'Yes, very well for the few hours since we went to bed. And you?'

'Not at all. I suppose I may have dozed off once or twice, but proper sleep, no. Every time I closed my eyes, I heard those terrible thuds as Tom Hunsey was being beaten to death. What am I going to tell the police, Rosa?' she asked in a suddenly urgent tone.

'That must depend on their line of questioning, but, in principle, as little as possible. I've been representing people long enough to know that the less one's clients say to the

72

police, the better. It's their job to try and get people to talk and they're pretty good at it, but it's not usually to the advantage of the person concerned.' She paused and gave Caroline a look of amazement. 'What on earth am I doing preaching to you? You who know even better than I the pitfalls of confession unless you have nothing whatsoever to hide, and not always then. How many people have you prosecuted to conviction who would have been acquitted if they'd not opened their mouths too wide? Not that you're in that category, though you do have a bit of explaining to do. As for the marks on your hand, I think you should stick to your story. Surely one of your plants is vicious enough to have scratched you. And if they ask you about the wet shoes in your cupboard, wouldn't it be reasonable that you arrived wearing them and changed in your office before presenting yourself at the party? After all, a good many of the female guests must have brought their party shoes tucked under their arms. Nobody's going to tiptoe through slush in high heels or a pair of open Gucci sandals.'

Caroline smiled. 'I never expected to hear you advise me on how to tell the police further lies.'

'That bit of advice comes from a friend, not from your solicitor,' Rosa said crisply.

After some further conversation, Caroline departed to have a bath and get dressed and at nine o'clock Peter Shoreham called for her in his car. Rosa remained out of sight indoors when he came, it having been agreed that Caroline would phone her from the office.

'Fortunately I have an outside line so can make calls without going through our switchboard,' she had said as she left the cottage.

'How are you feeling this morning?' Peter asked, casting her a worried glance as she got into the car.

'I'm all right. Have you heard any further news?'

'No. I tried to phone Charles Buck before I left home, but

Peggy answered and said he'd already gone.'

'I imagine we'll find the place teeming with police,' Caroline said without enthusiasm.

'They're bound to be nosing around for a day or two. I still hope it'll turn out to be an outside job.'

'But you don't seriously think it was, do you?'

'I'm afraid not,' Peter said with a heavy sigh.

'Presumably you have a theory about it?'

'I haven't and what's more I don't want to speculate. I hardly slept last night and I'm still stunned by what's happened.'

'Who would you like the murderer to turn out to be?' Caroline said, with a twisted smile.

'What a grotesque question!' he said in a shocked tone.

'I'm sorry. I shouldn't have said that. It was one of those remarks that came out wrong.'

'It's too horrible to contemplate that it might be anyone we know.'

They rounded a bend in the road and could see a number of police vehicles parked on the verge outside Grainfield Manor. A constable stood on duty by the entrance.

'We work here,' Peter said through the car window as he pulled up.

'Mind using the gate marked "exit", sir,' the officer said. 'I expect you've heard what happened last night?'

'We were both here,' Peter said, as he prepared to drive on.

'We must be the last to arrive,' Caroline observed wryly as they reached the staff car park and looked for a space. 'Do you think that looks suspicious?'

'I see Murray's here already,' Peter said.

'The good shepherd come to make sure that none of his flock are savaged by the big bad police,' Caroline said with a nervous laugh.

As they entered the house they found Chief Superintendent Tarr standing beside the doorkeeper's desk. Alec was talking to him and Tarr wore a frown and gave the occasional nod. Alec was the office know-all and, like all know-alls, distinctly loquacious.

'Good morning, Miss Allard,' Tarr said as Caroline walked past the desk. 'I'd like to have a word with you.'

He fell into step beside her as they reached the bottom of the staircase. Caroline bit her lip and looked round to Peter who was a few paces behind.

'Would you like me to come along too?' he asked. 'I'm sure Mr Tarr won't mind.'

'I'd sooner talk to Miss Allard alone,' Tarr said firmly. 'I think she might prefer it too.'

'Give me a buzz if you need me, Caroline,' Peter said in a tone that reflected his annoyance at Tarr's rebuff. 'I'll be in my room for half an hour before leaving for court.'

It had been on the tip of his tongue to make some snide comment about uniform chief superintendents taking charge of murder enquiries, but was immediately glad he had desisted. There was enough antagonism in the air without adding to it.

'There were just one or two things about last night I wanted to clear up,' Tarr said as he closed the door of Caroline's room behind him. 'I know you'll want to help the police in every way you can. Indeed, I know it'll be a relief to all of you to have the matter cleared up as soon as possible. I've spoken to Mr Riston who has given us a clear field in interviewing the members of his staff. I only mention that so you may know where we stand.'

'What is it you want to ask me?' Caroline said with a slight catch in her voice.

'I believe you told Inspector Bonham last night that you got the scratches on the back of your right hand when you were doing some indoor gardening.' He gave her a sardonic smile and nodded in the direction of the plants on her

75

window sill. 'I wonder if you'd show me which one it was that assaulted you.'

'I can't tell you which it was,' she said nervously. 'I only noticed it afterwards.'

'When would that have been?'

'Yesterday evening. As you're aware, I left the party and came to my room. While I was here I tended my plants.'

Tarr nodded and walked over to the window where he stared with an air of ostentatious concentration at the row of pots from which varieties of green foliage sprouted, trailed and thrust upwards.

'None of them looks particularly vicious to me. Which do you think it was?'

'I'm afraid I've no idea.'

'Has it happened before?'

'Often.'

'Long linear scratches like the one on the back of your right hand. Incidentally, I see it's almost healed. You've obviously put something on it.'

'Yes.'

'Very wise. Scratches can so easily turn septic,' he remarked in an urbane tone.

Caroline had always respected Tarr as a police officer without liking him. She was aware, too, that such respect was based on having hitherto been on the same side as he was. She now found, however, that her dislike bordered on hatred. He was showing himself to be a born bully who enjoyed playing cat and mouse with his victims.

'However,' he now went on, 'I gather you're certain you sustained those scratches in this room and not, for example, anywhere outside?'

'Of course I'm certain,' Caroline said with a deepening sense of dread.

'And I understand you told Mr Bonham that you never left your office yesterday evening between slipping away from

76

the party and being driven home by the Shorehams?'

'That's correct.'

'And it's the truth?' he asked with a mildly quizzical expression.

'Of course. Except . . .'

'Yes?' he said eagerly.

'What I told him was that I didn't leave my room after I got there. At that point I hadn't been driven home by the Shorehams.'

'One can always rely on you lawyers for accuracy,' Tarr observed drily. If not the truth, he reflected. I'm giving her every chance to come clean, but she's too frightened to tell me the truth. It has to be fear because she's not stupid. But what's she got to be afraid of?

'I think there's only one other thing, Miss Allard,' he said after a short silence. 'You keep a spare pair of shoes in that cupboard. Inspector Bonham noticed when he looked around your room after you'd gone that they had been recently worn. They were wet and there was some impacted snow round the edges. Can you explain that?'

'Very simply. I was wearing them when I arrived at the party and walked in them from where I parked the car. I was carrying my party shoes and changed here.'

'But you didn't reverse the procedure when you went home?'

Caroline felt her cheeks burning. 'It wasn't necessary,' she stammered. 'Mr Shoreham brought his car right up to the front door.'

Tarr observed her coolly. 'You seem to be finding our talk something of an ordeal, Miss Allard.'

'It's not pleasant being questioned about the murder of a colleague.'

'But surely if you're innocent and have nothing to hide . . .'

'I most certainly am innocent,' she broke in.

Ignoring the interruption he went on, 'Presumably you have your own theory as to Mr Hunsey's death. I should like to hear what you think – off the record if you prefer.'

'I have no theories at all,' she said.

'You can hardly expect me to believe that. The whole place must be rife with speculation.'

'If it is, I'm not privy to it. I think you're forgetting that I've been in your company ever since I arrived this morning, so haven't had an opportunity of talking to anyone apart from yourself.'

'Don't tell me you and Mr Shoreham didn't exchange views on your way here.'

'As a matter of fact we didn't.'

'Somebody had a motive for killing Mr Hunsey.'

'Obviously.'

'And that's all you can say to help the police? I'd have expected greater co-operation from someone on the staff of the Chief Prosecuting Solicitor.'

'I'm sorry.'

No you're not, he thought. You're stubborn, but above all you're frightened. He glanced again at the plants on the window sill. Then strolling over he brushed his hand through the foliage and examined the result with clinical interest.

'I'm afraid you've not seen the last of me, Miss Allard,' he remarked as he walked toward the door.

Caroline waited a full minute after his departure before dialling her cottage.

'Rosa, I can't stay here a minute longer, I'm coming back,' she said in a highly charged tone. 'I'll say I'm not feeling well.'

'I'll see you soon then,' Rosa said and rang off.

It was clearly not the moment for questions. As she awaited Caroline's return she wondered if, in similar circumstances, she might also have boxed herself in with lies

78

and reached the conclusion it was perfectly possible. Few people went through life without losing their heads at one time or another and anyone who did manage to do so was probably a pretty insufferable type.

She wandered into the kitchen. At least she could greet her friend with a cup of coffee on her return. Her friend who had overnight become her client.

CHAPTER THIRTEEN

Murray Riston had asked Charles Buck to come to his room for a discussion about the murder. Buck had waited ten carefully counted minutes before sauntering into the C.P.S.'s presence and taking up a position by the window from where he observed Murray with an air of detachment.

'You look as if you need your worry beads,' he remarked as he watched Murray fiddling with a rubber band.

Murray ignored the comment. 'I thought we ought to have a word about what's happened,' he said. 'I've been in touch with Tom Hunsey's sister in Northampton and expressed our horror and condolences. I gather the funeral will be there once the coroner releases the body. Naturally I shall attend on behalf of the department and I imagine some others may wish to come, too. But that's all looking to the future and it's the present I really wanted to discuss. I had a long talk with Tarr and Russell before I left here last night and assured them of our co-operation. I saw Tarr briefly when I arrived this morning and gathered there had been no overnight developments, which doesn't put us in a very happy position.' While he had been talking, Charles Buck had worn the air of someone who felt his time could be better spent elsewhere. 'I imagine the police have already interviewed you, Charles?' Murray went on. Buck gave a small nod, but said nothing. 'If you agree, I think you and I ought to keep one another in touch with anything either of us happens to learn,' he said in a tentative tone.

'I'm not so sure that I do agree,' Buck remarked, turning down the corners of his mouth as if Murray had made a particularly distasteful suggestion. 'Although you're the C.P.S., you can hardly presume to speak for everyone on the staff. It seems to me it's every man for himself, each of us being to some extent a suspect until an arrest has been made. Frankly, I don't see myself, in those circumstances, running to tell you every time I speak to the police or the police speak to me.' He gave Murray a smile that would have sent a kettle off the boil. 'After all, how do you know you're not looking at the murderer? Or vice versa for that matter?' He walked toward the door. 'I take it there was nothing else you wanted to say.'

Murray observed the retreating back of his deputy with a look of dispassion that belied his feelings. At least he now knew where the battle lines were drawn, Buck having shown how implacable he remained. He had never expected to win him over, for during the few weeks since he had taken up his appointment at Grainfield his deputy had made it clear that his allegiance was a formality and nothing more. But now it was as if Buck had openly declared war. If the murderer lay within their own ranks, there was no question of closing them and presenting the police with a united front of silence. Not that Murray had intended advocating such a course, but there were always the little things you didn't have to mention unless you were pressed.

He suddenly flicked the rubber band, with which he had been playing, across the room and watched it fall just where Buck had been standing. He decided his deputy wasn't as astute as he had previously believed. He had always given him credit for a certain native intelligence, but little of that had revealed itself during their recent conversation.

It could prove to be a dangerous game on which Buck had embarked, for though he, Murray Riston, had nothing to fear, could the same be said of his deputy?

Perhaps he ought, after all, to tell the police how he had seen him surreptitiously remove the murder weapon from Alec's desk and conceal it behind a curtain beside the front door.

CHAPTER FOURTEEN

Chief Superintendent Tarr and Detective Chief Inspector Russell sat in one of the police cars parked in the drive.

'I've just come from the mortuary,' Russell said. 'Dr Whittingham's view is that there was a severe blow to the front of the throat which fractured the thyroid cartilege and which was sufficient to have caused death. Thereafter he received at least three blows to the skull, each of which resulted in a fracture and an underlying contusion of the brain. So one way and another he was killed several times over. Whoever it was didn't mean him to get up and walk away.'

'Any fingerprints on the weapon?'

'A mass of smudged ones. Most of them probably Alec's. We've taken a set of his and will see how many we can eliminate. It may be necessary to fingerprint everyone who attended the party.'

'If we have to, we will,' Tarr said grimly. 'Starting with Miss Allard's.'

'We've got to find a motive,' Russell said with a sigh.

Tarr gazed out of the window at the rambling grey edifice that housed the C.P.S.'s staff. 'Clearly Tom Hunsey had found out something about somebody, but what?' he said angrily. 'We've got to establish a lead before we can hope to make any progress. At the moment it's like looking for a needle in a haystack.'

There was a silence, then Russell said, 'I'd always looked upon old Patching's staff as a fairly unexciting bunch. I never thought they'd produce a murder in their midst.'

'Bloody lawyers! As if they weren't enough nuisance anyway,' Tarr said with a harsh laugh. He rubbed his forehead. 'I'd hoped we might be able to identify some footprints at the scene.'

'The weather's been against us. The thaw's turned everywhere into a soggy mass. It's like putting your foot into a plate of runny stew.'

A moment or two later the eager face of Detective Constable Eagleford appeared at the car window. He had been deputed to assist the scene of crime officer and was clearly regarding it as a seat on a roller-coaster to accelerated promotion.

Tarr wound down the window. 'Why are you looking so pleased with yourself, Eagleford?' he enquired.

'I thought you'd want to know, sir, that we've found a couple of hairs on a bush close to where the body was. Actually, it was I who found them.' He peered from one officer to the other with an expectant expression.

'Well, go on,' Tarr said.

'They're long hairs. I'd say they were female hairs, sir.' With the air of a conjuror he suddenly produced a plastic envelope. 'Take a look for yourself, sir.'

'Could be Caroline Allard's,' Tarr remarked thoughtfully.

'I saw her leave in her car about fifteen minutes ago,' D.C. Eagleford said keenly.

Tarr and Russell exchanged a glance and got out of the car. With Eagleford bringing up the rear, they walked back toward the house.

CHAPTER FIFTEEN

Like many deputies appointments, Charles Buck's was for much of the time a non-job. When the C.P.S. was away, he functioned in his place, but otherwise it was up to the C.P.S. himself to use his deputy as much or as little as he pleased. Under Edward Patching he had become a sort of *eminence grise*. Patching had not really approved of the role, but had lacked the will to do anything about it. Moreover, Charles Buck was always ready to deal with disagreeable personnel problems from which Patching himself was apt to shrink.

With the arrival of Murray Riston, it soon became apparent that Charles Buck would be quietly shunted into oblivion. For the sake of appearances Murray was prepared to go through the motions of consulting him, but there was never any serious possibility of a harmonious working relationship, not least because Buck had put himself out on a limb.

Unless he had a luncheon engagement, it was Charles Buck's habit to drive to a pub called The Lamb which was situated about a mile and a half from Grainfield Manor. It was an unpretentious place where he would drink a pint of beer and eat a pork pie in the company of a handful of labourers from neighbouring farms, with whom he would exchange a few desultory observations on the weather, the crop prospects, or the current form of the pub's darts team.

On the day after Tom Hunsey's murder, however, he set

85

off in a different direction and twenty minutes later arrived outside Edward Patching's house. He had phoned in the course of the morning and proposed his visit.

Patching had not sounded too enthusiastic, but had acquiesced. Buck had offered to buy some food on his way, an offer which had been immediately accepted. Edward Patching had never been renowned for his liberality and retirement had seemingly made him even more frugal.

One of Buck's affectations, of which Patching had disapproved, was his very unlegal form of dress. If he was due to appear in court, he would put on a dark suit, but otherwise he tended to dress like a gentleman farmer at a local agricultural show. This involved wearing one or other of two brown suits, a striped shirt and his old rugby club tie, and either a fawn or a burgundy red camelhair waistcoat. A well-worn pair of suede shoes completed his attire. It was the shoes that had particularly affronted Edward Patching, who felt that lawyers on duty should always be shod in polished black leather.

'Hello, Edward, didn't mind my phoning, did you?' Buck said when the retired C.P.S. opened his front door. 'Thought I'd bring you the latest on last night's happening. Not that there's much to report. Riston's showing every sign of panic, but his type invariably fail in a crisis. I've made it plain that I'm not prepared to hold his hand while the police peck away like a lot of barnyard hens.'

Edward Patching closed the front door and threw a look of distaste at his visitor's back. There was so much about him that jarred. He could be brash and insensitive and would have made a disastrous C.P.S. It was fortunate, however, that he had no inkling that his ex-boss had put an effective spoke in his wheel with the committee of appointment. Not that he would have got the job even if Edward Patching had sung his praises to the sky. Only Charles Buck himself and his formidable wife and a few cronies had ever believed he

86

stood a chance.

'May I offer you a glass of sherry?' Patching said when they were in the living-room. 'It comes from Cyprus, but it's drinkable.'

'I won't say no, Edward. Incidentally, here are some scotch eggs I brought to help out.' He glanced around as if uncertain where to put his offering.

'I'll take them out to Alison. She's in the kitchen. I'm afraid we only have a snack at lunchtime.' Patching left the room, but returned a minute later. 'How's the enquiry going?' he said as he sat down.

'Tarr and Russell are both sure it must have been somebody who knew Hunsey and about whom Hunsey had discovered something to their discredit.'

'I gathered that much when Tarr was here last night. Incidentally, he seems to be running the show as if he were back in the C.I.D.'

'I know. But there's not much the hapless Russell can do about it.' Buck paused and went on in a significant voice, 'It's my belief, Edward, that the murder's connected with Riston's return to Grainfield. Nobody's going to persuade me that the two events are not related. It's too much of a coincidence to think otherwise.' Fixing Patching with a hard stare over the top of his spectacles he continued, 'And the third figure in the equation is that fellow Kline. I believe that Tom Hunsey with his nose for scandal managed to find out that Riston had behaved unprofessionally in relation to something his father-in-law had done. Something that would reflect so adversely on Riston's integrity that he would be obliged to resign.'

'You've canvassed all this before,' Patching said severely. 'You've absolutely no evidence. The matter you spoke about previously is dead and buried. Tarr said as much last night.'

Buck was silent for a while as he covertly studied the retired C.P.S. Then in an insinuating tone he said, 'That's not to say there isn't evidence to be found if one searches in the right place. This is where you come in, Edward.'

'I don't know what you mean. I think you'd better explain yourself rather carefully,' he said in the tone he normally reserved for anyone he suspected of taking liberties.

'Tarr will listen to you, Edward, whereas he won't pay any attention to what I tell him. He and I have never hit it off and anyway he thinks I have an axe to grind. It's up to you to give him the scent he's looking for.'

Edward Patching stared at his visitor in frank amazement.

'And what scent is that?' he asked disdainfully.

'To spend a day in our registry going through the files bearing Rex Kline's name.'

'Files?'

'Surely you know there's more than the one relating to the matter you mentioned to Tarr? He was reported for a traffic violation a few years ago, but no action was taken.'

'Oh?'

'It was on your advice, Edward.'

'I've no recollection of it,' Patching said dismissively. 'It can't have been very serious.'

'It wasn't.'

'I don't know why I should be expected to remember every traffic case in which I ever advised the police. They must have run into thousands.' His tone was biting, but Buck remained unruffled.

'There's a further file with Kline's name on it,' he now went on. 'An anonymous complainant wrote in saying he had signed a false declaration to assist a young man under age to obtain a passport.'

'Am I supposed to know about that?' Patching enquired in a withering tone.

'The file shows that Riston advised against any action.'

'So?'

'It's suspicious.'

'When did it happen?'

'Eight years ago.'

'Before, in fact, Rex Kline had become Murray Riston's father-in-law?'

'Even so.'

'Was there any evidence to justify further action?'

'The file was opened and closed on the same day. The police were never asked to make any enquiries.'

Patching plucked nervously at his lower lip. 'It seems to me, Charles, that you've allowed your dislike of Riston to colour your judgement. What Tarr is expected to glean from the files you've mentioned is beyond my comprehension. You're not seriously suggesting, are you, that a motive for Tom Hunsey's murder lies hidden away between their covers?'

'I'm suggesting that it's more likely to be found there than anywhere else. I'm positive that Riston is mixed up in it and, if I'm right about that, it's a fair inference it goes back to something he did when he was previously on the staff and which Tom Hunsey had sniffed out.'

'Tom may have taken an inordinate interest in scandal, but I'm certain he'd never have had the perseverance to read through old office files. It was hard enough to get him to apply his mind to his current work.'

'So you won't speak to Tarr?'

'I'm certainly not going to suggest he reads through the files you mention with a view to finding a motive to the murder. He knows all about the one matter – the allegation of bribery – and the other two are utterly trivial and can't possibly be relevant to his enquiry. Moreover, I think you'd be making a fool of yourself if you spoke to him. I strongly advise you not to do so. Personally I still hope the murderer will be found outside our own ranks. The alternative is too abhorrent to contemplate.'

'If you don't mind my saying so, Edward, I think you're

dwelling in cloud-cuckoo-land if you seriously believe that to be a possibility. However, I'm clearly not going to bring you round to my view, so I won't waste my breath further. Peggy'll be disappointed, too, that we don't see eye to eye on the best way to assist the police.'

Damn Peggy, Patching felt like saying. He realised that she felt even more venomous toward Murray Riston than her husband did. If they weren't careful, they might find themselves sued for defamation. Murray would be quite capable of issuing a writ.

When, however, Patching drew Buck's attention to this possibility if he didn't curb his tongue, Buck defiantly said that he'd welcome a writ as he could then publicly show up Grainfield's new C.P.S. for the man he was.

'I'd smash him and enjoy it,' he concluded in a tone that dared Patching to contradict him.

CHAPTER SIXTEEN

The atmosphere in Detective Chief Inspector Russell's office was stiflingly oppressive, which had nothing to do with the weather outside.

Russell sat at his desk with an air of palpable unease. A few feet away Tarr sat watchfully brooding as if biding his time to make a sudden pounce.

On the other side of the desk were Caroline Allard, bolt upright and stonily impassive, and next to her Rosa crouched forward in an attitude of imminent intervention.

It was all very well, Russell reflected, for Tarr to have assumed responsibility for Caroline's arrest, but he had insisted that Russell, as the C.I.D. officer in charge of the enquiry, should conduct the interview.

'We've just about got enough to arrest her,' he had said. 'We'll question her at the station, which'll be much more conducive to getting the truth out of her, and if at the end of it all we don't have sufficient to justify an immediate charge, she can be bailed under Section 43 of the Magistrates Courts Act 1980 which will give us time to decide what to do before she comes back in a couple of weeks' time.'

Russell had been frankly appalled by the proposal and by what he considered to be a cynical misuse of the provision in question. When he protested that it was the first time he had ever known the particular procedure to be used in a murder case, Tarr had blandly retorted that there had to be a first time for everything. When he went on to point out they were dealing with a professional person, namely a solicitor on the staff of the C.P.S., Tarr had merely shrugged and said sententiously that, as far as he was concerned, class and status were irrelevant in such matters. When Russell in final desperation suggested that they should seek a meeting with the D.P.P. in London and obtain his advice, Tarr had said they could do that later. Meanwhile they should get moving and apply for that warrant.

'Don't be so scared,' he had said. 'We'll cover ourselves all along the line.' Then in a revealing moment he had added, 'If we pussyfoot around this enquiry, our reputations will be nil. There we were guests at the very party where the murder was committed and on the scene almost before the victim expelled his last breath and yet we allowed ourselves to become bogged down through fear of taking a wrong step.'

'I still think we ought to be a bit cautious . . .' Russell had begun.

'Caution's one thing, timidity's another and nobody's yet ever accused me of being timid,' Tarr had said emphatically.

What neither he nor Russell had foreseen, however, was that Caroline already had a legal adviser at her side. Accordingly, it was to Russell's dismay and Tarr's annoyance that Rosa had accompanied her client to the police station and was now giving the impression of merely waiting for the police to make a false move.

'I want to give you the opportunity of explaining one or two matters, Miss Allard,' Russell said, nervously clearing his throat.

'Aren't you forgetting that my client is in custody and that you have cautioned her?' Rosa broke in. 'She has no further explanations to give at this stage.'

'Nevertheless, I feel I have a duty to ask her if she would care to explain how hairs, which match her own, came to be found on a bush at the scene of the murder.'

Caroline shook her head numbly and Rosa said, 'On my advice Miss Allard is keeping her explanations to herself for the time being.'

Tarr stirred impatiently in his chair. 'You don't seem to appreciate, Miss Epton, that we are bending over backwards to be fair to Miss Allard and to give her every opportunity of explaining the various points that seem to tell against her.'

'Your sense of fairness is a matter of opinion,' Rosa retorted crisply.

Tarr frowned. Until this day he had neither met nor heard of Rosa Epton, a state of affairs he'd have been happy to see continue. He was acquainted with all the local solicitors and felt he knew how to handle them. Moreover, they were all male. But this slip of a girl with her elfin face and her hair which she was constantly pushing back over her ears was something new in his experience. His initial paternal approach had been a dismal failure.

'Miss Allard, you and I have known each other for a good many years,' he said, ignoring Rosa and fixing Caroline with a benign, yet slightly reproachful look. 'We have worked together and, I like to think, held one another in mutual respect; so I hope you believe me when I say that I derive no pleasure from this interview. Indeed, I find it most distasteful, as does Chief Inspector Russell . . .'

'But it didn't stop you arresting her,' Rosa broke in. After a pause she went on, 'What I'm really saying, Mr Tarr, is cut the soft talk. It's not the right occasion. As I've made clear, Miss Allard doesn't wish to say anything at this juncture. It's her right to remain silent. That's what the caution is all about in case you've forgotten. So either charge her or release her.'

Rosa's tone was as challenging as her expression and Tarr glared at her angrily. He motioned Russell to follow him and the two officers left the room.

Caroline immediately sagged in her chair and gave Rosa a wan smile.

'Round one to us,' Rosa said robustly. 'If I'm not mistaken, we'll shortly be on our way home. It was a diabolical liberty arresting you and we're going to make sure it backfires on him.'

'Nevertheless the damage has been done,' Caroline said forlornly. 'The publicity will destroy me whatever happens.'

'It mayn't be as bad as you fear,' Rosa observed.

'Don't let's fool ourselves! It will be.'

'All that talk about being fair!' Rosa said vehemently. 'They're like large dogs that sweep cherished ornaments off tables with a wave of their tails. They're so used to arresting people and carting them off to police stations that they never pause to consider the consequences when they subsequently let the person go. They simply don't realise the anxiety and distress they cause innocent people. To them, being arrested should be no more than a minor inconvenience. A mere hiccough in your life.'

'They don't really believe anyone they question is actually innocent,' Caroline remarked bitterly. Suddenly she braced herself as the door opened and the two officers came in.

'If you'll just sign the bail form and report back in two weeks time, that'll be all for the time being, Miss Allard,' Russell said in a carefully casual voice.

'As you'll know,' Tarr added, 'when you return to the station you will either be charged or your recognisance will be discharged.'

Caroline gave a brief nod and picked up her handbag from the floor.

'I'll see you out,' Russell said. As they walked along the corridor he seemed about to say something but suddenly refrained. His discomfort throughout the interview had been most marked and it was clear that Tarr had been the instigator of what had happened. Rosa wondered how he would account to his superiors, but realised everything would depend on events during the next two weeks.

He was likely to use the time in an aggressive search for further evidence which would justify the police charging Caroline with murder on her next appearance. After all, his own reputation was very much at stake.

It was a thought, the full implication of which chilled her as she followed Caroline out of the police station.

CHAPTER SEVENTEEN

'How nice to meet you again, Rosa!' Murray Riston said in his friendliest manner as he greeted her at the door of his room and led her to his visitor's chair. 'It's been a long time.'

He showed no sign of embarrassment that though Caroline was once more the cause of their meeting, it was in very different circumstances from the previous occasions, both of which Rosa had recalled as she drove to Grainfield Manor on the morning after Caroline's arrest.

The first had been when the three of them had dined at an Italian restaurant near Rosa's flat and Caroline had proudly introduced Murray to her. The second, a few months later, was when they went to a concert at the Festival Hall together. Rosa had somehow managed to get tickets for one of the rare appearances of the Berlin Philharmonic. It had been a Brahms evening of such uplifting spirituality that none of them had wanted to talk afterwards. She wondered, as she sat down, if Murray remembered the two occasions as clearly as she did. It had been six years ago, but he had hardly changed. A few grey hairs at the temple, but that was about all. The youthful figure and the boyish expression were still intact.

'How is Caroline?' he asked earnestly. 'Is she bearing up O.K? She did understand that I had no option but to suspend her until this ghastly business has been resolved? Not that anyone's going to persuade me that Caroline murdered Tom

Hunsey.'

Rosa found herself once more wondering how far she trusted him. She still had the same doubts from when she first met him. She had phoned the previous evening to say she would like to come and talk to him and he had responded with alacrity and said how glad he was that she had called.

'Did Tarr tell you he was going to arrest her?' Rosa asked curiously.

Murray nodded and looked embarrassed. 'I was dumb-founded and could scarcely believe my ears.'

'He seems to have acted in an extremely high-handed manner,' Rosa said. 'Not to mention an extremely unorthodox one.'

'That's Bernard Tarr. He's nobody's fool, though he is apt to rush in where angels would fear to tread.'

'But you don't believe Caroline did it?'

'I *can't* believe it,' he said in an anguished voice. 'And, anyway, where's the motive?'

'Exactly. There isn't one.'

'Well, then . . .' He let the sentence tail away. A moment later he went on, 'I'm so glad she has you looking after her interests, Rosa. It really is a relief knowing that. She couldn't be in better hands.' He paused and picked up the elegant silver paperknife that lay beside the leather blotter on his desk. 'The staff presented me with this when I left to go up north,' he said as he studied its sharp tip. In a sad tone he went on, 'I'd have given anything for this not to have happened. It's almost as if a curse has been put on my return here.'

'It's certainly an unhappy start to your reign,' Rosa remarked. Like most men in her experience, he was obviously a prey to self-pity, but he could hardly expect her to provide balm in the circumstances. 'Do you take the view that the murderer must have been known to Mr Hunsey?'

'It's the obvious inference, I'm afraid.'

'And therefore it was somebody on the staff here?'

'Not necessarily. There were a number of guests at the party who knew him.'

'Even so, it must have been somebody who saw him leave the house and who followed him. Somebody who was so alarmed that murder became an urgent necessity.'

'I know! But what on earth could Tom have said to the murderer to have caused that result? Of course Tarr's theory is that it was Tom who followed Caroline and she who suddenly turned and killed him.'

'Having armed herself in advance with a lethal weapon,' Rosa commented sarcastically. 'It just doesn't make sense, does it?'

'I agree. But don't underestimate Tarr. He'll leave no stone unturned to try and prove what he believes happened.'

'And I shall leave no stone unturned to confound him,' Rosa retorted. 'I think it's absolutely disgraceful what he's done. He's effectively destroyed Caroline's professional life and maybe done even worse than that. Surely you must feel equally strongly about it, Murray?'

'Indeed; I think it was most ill-judged.'

'Ill-judged!'

'Please, Rosa, I know what you're thinking, but I am the Chief Prosecuting Solicitor and I can hardly launch a public campaign on behalf of one of my staff whom the police have arrested. Privately I'm entirely on Caroline's side, but publicly I have to show a certain amount of circumspection.' He gave her a pleading look. 'I'm sure you understand my position. But having said that, tell me in what way you think I can help Caroline's cause.'

'Presumably you have your own ideas about who killed Tom Hunsey?'

'I'm genuinely and totally mystified. I really mean that, Rosa.' He paused and gazed across the expanse of his large office. 'I have wondered if we're not all barking up the wrong tree. By which I mean that Tom's murder might not have had anything to do with his nose for scandal.'

'So?'

He gave a quick, slightly impatient shake of his head. 'That's all! I don't have any ready-made alternative. But that doesn't mean there isn't one. Merely that nobody has yet had the wit to perceive it.'

Rosa stared at him stonily. For a moment she had thought he was about to voice a new theory that would give her something on which to work. Instead, his words had been as meaningless as those of a preacher seeking to explain the inexplicable.

'It seems to me,' she said firmly, 'that until some totally new line opens up, we must accept that it was Hunsey's penchant for scandal that led to his death. It's a question of finding out who had a motive.'

Murray nodded eagerly. 'It all comes back to motive.'

'It's inconceivable,' Rosa went on, 'that there isn't somebody who can't throw some light on that aspect if he wished to.'

'If I could, I certainly would,' Murray said quickly. Then giving Rosa a fraught glance, he added, 'If only to clear the air around my own head. All sorts of rumours are flying about, some of which affect me personally. They're scurrilous and totally unjustified and they don't make my job at all easy. Nevertheless, I don't intend to let them undermine my authority as C.P.S. As Caroline will have told you, I've not come back to a very contented department, but I'd hoped to make things better. But now with this ghastly business . . .'

'Would Tom Hunsey have made real enemies?' Rosa asked after a silence.

'He wasn't a particularly likeable person and at best was tolerated by his colleagues, but I don't know about actual enemies. I suspect he was probably a lonely person.

Sometimes he would excite one's pity, but as soon as you helped him you'd wonder why you'd taken the trouble. He wasn't without touches of kindness, but I doubt whether he knew what magnanimity was. He could also become quite upset and emotional on occasions.'

'Caroline mentioned an incident when a cyclist was knocked over and killed by a hit and run motorist near his home. She said how it had preyed on his mind.'

'I seem to remember hearing about that,' Murray remarked vaguely.

'I take it you won't mind my talking to your staff?' Rosa said.

'It's up to you, Rosa, who you talk to. I doubt whether the police'll be very happy about it, however. They've interviewed everyone here in the course of their enquiries and you know how they feel about interference with witnesses.'

'All too well! They always think they have a sole proprietary right in anyone they've interviewed. One can't disabuse them often enough. Witnesses are one thing, people from whom they've taken statements are in a quite different category.' She gave Murray an apologetic smile. 'I'm sorry, I didn't mean to lecture you. But to talk about witnesses in the present instance is rubbish when they don't even have a case under way. Nobody's yet been charged with any offence.'

Murray was silent for a moment. Then suddenly standing up, he said, 'It's been lovely seeing you again, Rosa. Don't hesitate to get in touch with me if there's anything I can properly do for Caroline. I pray it won't be long before she's in the clear. If you want to talk to other members of the staff while you're here, why don't you start with Charles Buck? I know he's in this morning and I'll get my secretary to take you along to his room.'

Rosa knew enough not to be surprised that he didn't offer to escort her himself.

'So you're the Miss Epton who's the scourge of the Metropolitan Police,' Buck observed in a heavily facetious tone as he waved Rosa to sit down, at the same time gazing at her over the top of his spectacles with an air of masculine superiority. Rosa blinked in faint surprise and Buck went on in the same heavy tone, 'You see your reputation has even reached us rustics in Grainfield. But am I not right in thinking you once appeared before our local justices?'

'Yes.'

'I thought so. A motoring case in which Caroline prosecuted?'

'Yes.'

'Portia against Portia,' he remarked with a pleased smile. 'But tell me, Miss Epton, what brings you to my room?'

'I'm here as Caroline's solicitor.'

'That much I gathered.'

'Do you think she's guilty?'

'I have no idea what evidence they possess.'

'All right, perhaps I asked the wrong question. Can you suggest any motive Caroline might have had for the murder?'

'Ah! *Cherchez le motif!* I'm afraid I have no knowledge of motive on the part of anyone. No knowledge at all.'

'Would you be prepared to speculate for my benefit?'

'I think it would be highly dangerous to do so,' he said in a tone that implied he had trumped her ace.

'If you did feel free to speculate, would Caroline figure in your speculation?'

'She would not,' he replied in a deliberately teasing voice.

'Do you not feel outraged by what the police have done?'

'I'm far too old a hand in the law to be outraged by anything, Miss Epton. It's a long time since I displayed anything but forensic outrage and that's strictly reserved for court.'

'Do you yourself believe that the murderer must have been

101

known to Hunsey?'

'Naturally.'

'Is there anything at all you can tell me that will help Caroline?' Rosa asked urgently.

'I'm afraid you're knocking on the wrong door, Miss Epton.' He blew out his cheeks and gazed at her with the same air of masculine superiority he had shown throughout. Rosa had the impression that he had regarded their talk as in the nature of a fencing match. Suddenly he said, 'Is Caroline going away for Christmas?'

'I wanted her to come and spend it with me in London, but she doesn't wish to go away until things have been settled one way or another.'

'Will you be staying with her?'

'Yes.'

He nodded as if finding this a satisfactory state of affairs. Rosa, for her part, had been shocked by the way Caroline's colleagues had reacted to her arrest and release on bail. Apart from the Shorehams, none of them had done more than make cautiously sympathetic noises. It was as if they feared coming out in spots from closer contact.

Rosa normally spent Christmas with her father at his country rectory in Herefordshire, but he had died the previous summer and, with her only brother living in America, she had no immediate family with whom to spend the holiday. She had been invited to spend Christmas day with the Snaiths. Robin was her partner and lived with his wife, three children and an assortment of animals in a charming old farm house whose chimney pots were skimmed every time planes took off and landed on one of Heathrow's main runways. She had phoned Robin to ask if it would be all right to bring Caroline with her for the day, but later had to explain that her friend declined to leave home and to say she felt she ought to stay with her.

She had reorganised her own work schedule for the next

102

couple of weeks and had paid a number of flying visits to London to deal with matters requiring her attention. For the time being her place, both as a friend and as a professional adviser, was at Caroline's side. Caroline herself said little, but Rosa knew she was grateful.

As she left Charles Buck's office, she passed Chief Superintendent Tarr at the top of the stairs. He seemed taken aback at seeing her and gave her a disapproving frown.

'Perhaps you can tell me where I can find Mr Ives, the chief clerk?' she said with a note of challenge in her tone.

'I suggest you ask the doorman,' he replied tartly. 'But I think I ought to warn you that he will be a prosecution witness and it would be better if you didn't talk to him.'

'Better for whom?' Rosa enquired. 'In any event, he can scarcely be labelled prosecution witness when you've not yet charged anyone with an offence.'

Tarr seemed about to take up her challenge, then shrugged and said, 'As long as you appreciate the risks, Miss Epton; namely, that you could later be accused of interfering with a witness.'

'I'll cope with that accusation when the time comes,' Rosa remarked. 'I never look for a fight with the police, but equally I never run away from one. And now, if you'll excuse me, I'll go and find Mr Ives.'

'Mr Ives, miss?' Alec, the doorman repeated when Rosa asked for directions. 'Down that passage and it's the third door on the left. What used to be the butler's pantry. You're Miss Allard's lawyer, aren't you, miss? Very sorry about her trouble, particularly as she'd never have murdered Mr Hunsey. It may look black against her, but she never did it. You know the murderer had the brass to use my ruler? Ought to have hidden it, but I didn't. It was given me for my protection, not for murdering innocent folk.'

Satisfied that he had temporarily run out of words, Rosa said, 'Why are you so certain that Miss Allard's innocent?'

'She's not the murdering sort,' Alec remarked with authority. In a confiding tone, he added, 'Anyway who ever heard of a woman bashing out a fellow's brains? It's not their way.'

Rosa nodded at this not wholly convincing statement. 'Who do you think did do it?' she asked hopefully.

Alec glanced quickly about him before lowering his voice and saying, 'He loved a bit of scandal, did Mr Hunsey. Often tried to find out what I'd picked up, not that I ever told him anything. I could have, mind you. Sitting here, you hears all sorts of things. Things which are best kept to oneself.' He gave her a conspiratorial wink. 'You know what I'm talking about, don't you, miss?'

'I'm sure you're the soul of discretion,' Rosa said tactfully.

'I could make your ears flap like blankets drying in a wind if I wanted to,' he said, eyeing Rosa with a slightly lecherous expression.

'I'd be grateful if you'd tell me anything which could help Miss Allard,' Rosa said, moving back a step. One of his hands had already brushed against her thigh and lingered on its return journey.

'Miss Allard never murdered him,' he said, shaking his head at the apparent absurdity of the idea.

'I know she didn't, but someone did,' Rosa observed with a touch of impatience.

'Why do you think it happened just after Mr Riston arrived and Mr Patching departed?'

'You tell me.'

'Who was furious he didn't get the job?'

'I understand Mr Buck was upset,' Rosa said cautiously.

'Upset! He blew his top he was so angry. And when Mr Buck gets angry, there's quite a scene, I can tell you.'

'But why should Mr Buck kill Mr Hunsey?' Rosa asked, aware of the enormity of her question, but not caring.

'Because Mr Hunsey had found out something about him,

that's why.'

'What?'

'Ah! Now that's asking! You discover that and you'll solve the case.'

'You must have some idea to have suggested it,' Rosa urged.

'Oh, I have an idea all right, but I'm not saying, am I?'

'Not even to save Miss Allard from being charged with murder?'

'I've said too much already,' he remarked with a worried shake of his head.

Rosa forebore to point out that he had virtually said nothing at all. It had been like so much candy floss.

'I wish you luck, miss,' he went on. 'I liked Miss Allard. She and me always got on. I wouldn't have minded having her as a daughter.' He glanced past Rosa. 'There's Mr Ives . . . Hey, George, this young lady wants to have a word with you.'

George Ives looked at Rosa in alarm.

'I'm afraid I'm rather busy at the moment, Miss . . .'

'Epton.'

'Yes, of course. I heard your name mentioned yesterday.'

'If you could spare me just a few minutes, I'd be grateful,' Rosa said.

George Ives gazed at her with indecision. Eventually he said in a tone of considerable reluctance, 'I really am very busy and I don't think there's anything I can properly tell you at this stage. However, if you like to come to my office just for a minute we can have a quick word, but I'm afraid it can't be more than that.' He led the way down a passage and fumbled to unlock a door at the end. 'The police have advised me to keep my door locked,' he murmured. 'You see, I have all the staff files in my office.' He ushered Rosa in and closed the door firmly behind him. 'These old houses make wretched offices,' he remarked. 'This used to be the

105

butler's pantry.'

'So your man on the door told me. It's certainly more appropriate for polishing silver than poring over files,' Rosa observed with a quick smile as she took in her surroundings. 'It makes my office in London seem like a drawing room by comparison.'

'I'm afraid we lack clout with the local authority when it comes to accommodation,' Ives said in a resigned tone. 'Also, Mr Patching wasn't forceful enough when it came to arguing about such matters with the powers that be. If it had been left to Mr Buck, we'd probably have been in a brand new building by now. However, I'm hoping Mr Riston will take up the cudgels on our behalf. I know he thinks we've been treated shabbily in this respect.'

Rosa gave a quick nod in the hope of cutting off further reflections on the inadequacy of the C.P.S.'s accommodation. If George Ives could spare her only a few minutes she didn't wish to spend them listening to his grumbles. Her suspicion that it could be a ploy on his part to forestall her asking him embarrassing questions was soon to be confirmed.

'There are two reasons why I can't talk freely to you, Miss Epton,' he said abruptly. 'The first is that I am bound to be a prosecution witness as I was the person who found the body. Therefore it would not be proper for me to talk to the defence.'

'But at the moment there is no prosecution,' Rosa broke in. 'Nobody's been charged.'

'Nevertheless . . .' he said with a worried frown. 'And, anyway, equally important is the fact that I couldn't possibly talk to you without Mr Riston's permission.'

'Phone him and ask him if he objects,' Rosa said.

'It's not a matter that can be dealt with by a quick phone call.'

'Let me speak to him then.'

He shook his head. 'You have to accept my judgement in the matter, Miss Epton.'

Rosa bit her lip. Short of seizing his phone and asking to be connected with the C.P.S., there was nothing further she could do.

George Ives glanced at his watch and stood up. He's as prim and fussy as the white rabbit in Alice in Wonderland, Rosa reflected.

'May I ask you one question before I go?' she asked.

He looked immediately apprehensive. 'I can't promise to answer it.'

'Have you said anything at all to the police that is to Miss Allard's disadvantage?'

'My statement to the police was entirely factual,' he said warily.

'Does Miss Allard's name appear in it?'

'Only in a negative sense. They asked me if I'd seen her at the time I discovered the body and I said I hadn't. Now, I really must go, Miss Epton. I'm late for an appointment and I've already said more than I should.'

He opened the door and Rosa got up. With an air of considerable firmness he escorted her to the front door. Alec was taking delivery of a sack of mail as she passed his desk and was laboriously signing his name in the postman's register. He didn't look up and Rosa, after a second's hesitation, decided not to distract him.

'I'll sign you out, Miss Epton,' Ives said, as though he read her thoughts, and almost pushed her through the door.

For a while she sat in her car and gazed at the house. From where she had parked it resembled architectural chaos with additions and outbuildings seemingly stuck on at random. Its occupants appeared to be equally at odds with one another, she reflected, as she started the engine and headed back for Caroline's cottage.

She found Caroline in the kitchen making a Christmas

107

pudding.

'I know it's a bit late in the day,' Caroline remarked, 'but if it's inedible, the birds can have it. Or I might even save it for next Christmas. Perhaps they'll let you come and share it with me in my open prison.'

'Don't be so morbid!' Rosa said.

'I was trying to be realistic. Anyway, how was your morning at the manor? Whom did you see?'

'If you'll come and sit down, I'll tell you. Bring that brandy with you, too.'

'You think we're more deserving than the pudding?'

'I don't want to spoil your fun, but I bought a Christmas pudding when I was in town yesterday. It's upstairs wrapped in an old scarf. Now will you come and sit down?'

Rosa had completed her recital of the morning's events before noticing that Caroline had almost finished off the brandy.

'It's no good, Rosa,' she said with a heavy sigh as tears began to trickle down her cheeks, 'even your best can't save me. I might as well lie back and let the waves sweep over me.'

'The only waves sweeping over you have come out of that bottle. Once their effect has passed, we're going to have a long talk. A long solicitor client talk.'

CHAPTER EIGHTEEN

Like all autocrats, Chief Superintendent Tarr had a pronounced sense of vanity and, like all vain men, if there was one thing he disliked above any other, it was to be put on the mat and dressed down.

Accordingly he emerged from his meeting with the Assistant Chief Constable not so much chastened as smarting. He was determined, however, not to let anybody have the satisfaction of knowing how sore he felt.

The Assistant Chief, who had overall responsibility for C.I.D. operational matters, had demanded to know what he thought he was up to taking into custody someone on the C.P.S.'s staff and then bailing her under Section 43 of the Magistrates' Courts Act? Either he had sufficient evidence to charge her, which he clearly had not, or it was plainly a case for consulting him, the Assistant Chief, and probably the D.P.P., neither of which he had done. Moreover, the Assistant Chief had gone on, what was he, a uniformed Chief Superintendent, doing meddling in a C.I.D. matter?

The word 'meddling' had particularly stung Tarr and he had hotly pointed out that he was the senior officer present when the murder was discovered; that he, better than any other officer, knew the C.P.S.'s staff; and that as the chief superintendent in charge of a district he had a responsibility for the C.I.D. officers serving therein.

This last point was his strongest, for though the C.I.D.

had its own operational chain of command up to the Detective Chief Superintendent at headquarters and through him to the Assistant Chief Constable as general overlord of all C.I.D. matters, it had always been accepted that the uniformed Chief Superintendents in each district exercised a measure of responsibility for C.I.D. officers serving in their district. Personal inclination was the deciding factor. One or two simply didn't want to know what their C.I.D. officers got up to, whereas others, of whom Tarr was one, maintained a vigilant eye on their detectives, often to the discomfiture of the senior C.I.D. man in post. In Tarr's district, this was the hapless Detective Chief Inspector Russell.

As Tarr drove back to his own headquarters in the centre of Grainfield, he burned with resentment and with an even stronger determination to unearth such further evidence as would justify his charging Caroline with murder when she answered to her bail.

He was certain of her guilt (why should she tell lies if she was innocent?) and was impatient of anything that didn't fit in with this belief.

Not long after his return to his office, he received a call from Murray Riston. It came through on their direct line and informed him in the most confidential tone how the C.P.S. had seen his deputy surreptitiously remove the murder weapon from Alec's desk and conceal it behind a curtain. This item of information brought forth only a grudging acknowledgment, for in no way could it be seen to fit his conception of what had happened. Unless, of course, Caroline Allard had also witnessed the move . . .

'I'm sure there's a perfectly innocent explanation,' Murray had hastened to say in a tone that clearly implied he hoped there wasn't, 'but I thought I ought to mention it.'

Tarr said unenthusiastically that he, too, was sure it had an innocent explanation. He forbore to ask the C.P.S. why he had not mentioned it earlier.

As he sat quietly fuming, there was a knock on the door and Detective Chief Inspector Russell came in.

'We're not going to get anywhere until we've uncovered a motive,' Russell said with the air of a dejected bloodhound.

'I know, so don't go on saying it,' Tarr snapped. After a pause he went on, 'The Allard girl must have some skeleton hidden away in a cupboard, which the nosey Hunsey discovered. The question is what sort of skeleton is it?'

'Something to do with one of her cases,' Russell put in on cue.

'That's the most likely,' Tarr said with a satisfied nod. 'Has there ever been any hint of scandal involving the girl?'

Russell shook his head gloomily. 'Not that I've heard of.'

'I wonder if she ever did a cover-up for Murray Riston? I wonder . . . I wonder . . . The occasion when it was suggested that Riston had used his position to help Rex Kline out of a difficulty, I wonder if Caroline Allard ought to have come under closer scrutiny.' He became thoughtful and it was half a minute before he spoke again. 'She's a single girl in her thirties with no private means. I've found that out. She's therefore totally dependent on her job for money. It would be a disaster for her if she lost it. In those sort of circumstances murder might not seem too high a price to pay for her security.' He gave Russell a sudden hard stare. 'That's the line we've got to investigate. Put every available man on to it. We have just one week to discover her motive. It's there waiting to be dug up. Let's waste no more time.'

Russell left Tarr's office gloomier than he had entered it. He felt like someone cut off by a rising tide. The only thing in doubt was exactly how high it would rise.

CHAPTER NINETEEN

For several days Rex Kline, normally one of nature's extroverts, had been moody and preoccupied. The fact that he denied anything was wrong deceived nobody, least of all his wife.

'I'm going into town to do some Christmas shopping,' Molly Kline said in a coaxing tone. 'Why don't you come? You could help me choose some presents.'

He shook his head. 'I'm not in the mood for shopping and you know I hate the crowds. Anyway, I've got some business correspondence to attend to.'

His wife let out a quiet sigh. 'Don't forget that Jennifer and Murray are coming to supper this evening.'

'Why should I forget?' he asked a trifle testily.

'I thought I'd just remind you.'

'And now you have.' He contrived to give her a smile. 'Don't look so worried, Molly,' he added. 'I'll be here when you get back.'

'I'm only worried because I can tell that you're worried.'

'I've had business worries before. They're part of my life.'

'Are they only business worries?'

'Of course. It's just that they've hit me when I was feeling a bit off colour anyway.'

Molly looked at him doubtfully. She was sure he wasn't telling her the truth, but she knew from experience that nothing she could say would elicit more.

'All right, I'll leave you in peace,' she said in a still worried tone, kissing him lightly on the cheek. 'I shan't be gone more than a couple of hours.'

'It'll take you longer than that to fight your way to the first counter,' he remarked with a forced laugh. Observing her expression, he propelled her gently toward the door. 'Off you go! I promise I'll be here when you get back. I'm not going to be kidnapped by a team of reindeer.'

It was no good his telling her not to worry, Molly reflected as she set out on the five miles drive into Grainfield, she *was* worried. And the fact that his present state dated from that horrendous Christmas party did nothing to lessen her feeling of apprehension.

She was devoted to her husband and had always been very much a home-maker. She was the perfect wife for Rex, who was thoroughly outgoing and forever bursting with ideas for making money. She would listen attentively to as much as he told her, though she had little interest in the details of his business activities. So long as he was happy she was content and asked no questions.

Jennifer was their only child (a son born earlier had died at birth, to Molly's lasting grief) and it had delighted both her parents when she became engaged to Murray Riston after only a short acquaintance. Molly's initial reservation about their age difference had been quickly dispelled by Murray's boyish charm. Rex recognised in his future son-in-law all the qualities of drive and determination he saw in himself. Their happiness had been further enhanced when Murray applied for the post of C.P.S. at Grainfield and was duly appointed. The fact that he and Jennifer and their small granddaughter would be living nearby filled them with pleasure, Molly because she was a doting grandmother, and Rex because (in part at any rate) he was one of nature's fixers and liked to be personally acquainted with anyone holding an important position. He wouldn't, however, have admitted it in quite such crude terms.

But now as Molly drove into Grainfield to do her shopping it seemed to her that a large black cloud had anchored itself over their lives. Rex had become morose and was completely out of sorts and Murray was clearly desperately worried by what had happened. And small wonder! What should have been an auspicious and enjoyable occasion had turned into grim tragedy. It was grossly unfair on him that he should have been plunged into this terrible atmosphere in which suspicion found such a fertile breeding ground.

Molly had never given much thought to murder before, but now she execrated it for disrupting her domestic harmony.

Not long after she had left the house that afternoon, her husband picked up the phone and dialled a local number.

'I've been thinking things over and we ought to meet,' he said when a voice answered. 'Know what I'm referring to? Good! Better not say any more on the phone. Let's make it same place as last time. Six o'clock all right? It'll be dark by then, so quite safe.'

He glanced at his watch. Molly wouldn't be home before five at the earliest, but he had better be out of the house before then. He didn't want to have to go into explanations. Particularly false ones.

Picking up the receiver again he dialled his daughter's number. It was engaged and he waited a few minutes before trying again.

'Jennie, it's me. Your mother's gone shopping and left me alone in the house, so I thought I'd give you a call. We're looking forward to seeing you for supper this evening. What time are you coming?'

'Murray's just phoned from the office. He says he'll be late getting home. It means we shan't be with you till after eight.'

'That'll be all right.'

'I'm so worried about Murray. This murder enquiry is

really getting him down. The atmosphere at the Manor is unbelievably nasty. He's trying so hard to be his normal buoyant self, but the strain's beginning to tell. The fact that Caroline Allard has been arrested seems to have done nothing to clear the air. If they think she did it, I don't understand why she hasn't been charged.'

'I know, it's all very bewildering to the layman, but let's hope it'll be settled quite soon. My own source of information is that the police are likely to charge her.'

'Poor girl!' Jennifer said in a heartfelt tone. 'Murray feels particularly bad about it.'

'You can't afford to be sentimental in these matters. In any event it's going to be a forbidden subject when we're together this evening, I promise you that.'

With the call over he sank slowly into a chair and closed his eyes. His son-in-law wasn't the only person under strain.

CHAPTER TWENTY

'I can't think what's happened to Rex,' Molly Kline said to her daughter at half past eight that evening.

She had arrived home around five-thirty to find the house empty. As he often went out without leaving a note she didn't worry, assuming he would be back by seven at the latest. When he wasn't, she rang Jennifer who told her that she and her father had spoken on the phone earlier in the afternoon when she had informed him that Murray was going to be late home.

'Murray should be here any minute now,' Jennifer observed as she and her mother sat in the drawing-room awaiting their menfolk. 'When he called me the second time he said I should come on ahead as he was going to be kept later than he'd expected.'

'I suppose it's to do with this ghastly business,' Molly remarked with a shiver.

'Probably. He didn't say and I didn't ask him. He no longer tells me everything the way he used to.'

'I'm sure that's just a temporary thing, darling. You must make allowances for him.'

'I do.'

'Of course you do,' Molly said affectionately. She let out a sigh and added, 'Well, there's only one thing we can do and that's have another drink. And I'd better turn down the oven or our supper will only be fit for compost.'

Half an hour and two drinks later the phone rang. The two women exchanged glances of mutual apprehension. Molly got up and went into the hall to answer it.

'It's me, Molly,' her son-in-law said as soon as he heard her voice.

'Where are you, Murray? We were beginning to get worried.'

'I've only just got home. The thing is, Molly, I'm feeling completely knackered, so will you excuse me if I don't come? All I want is to go straight to bed. Please explain to Jennifer and make my apologies to Rex.'

'Don't you want to speak to Jennifer yourself?'

'No, you explain,' he said in an exhausted voice.

'Rex isn't home yet,' Molly said anxiously. 'You don't know where he is?'

'I've no idea. Probably his car's broken down.'

'Then why hasn't he phoned?'

'I'm sure there's no need to worry, Molly . . .'

It was at this point that Jennifer came into the hall and held out a hand for the receiver.

'Jennifer's beside me and wants to have a word with you,' Molly said abruptly.

'What's happened, darling?' Jennifer asked. 'Why are you phoning? Why aren't you here?'

'I've just explained to your mother. I've arrived home totally exhausted and am going straight to bed. I'm terribly sorry, but I'm no company for anybody this evening. I'll probably be asleep by the time you get back.'

'But where have you been? What's held you up?'

'I've been working, love, what do you think I've been doing?' he replied with a touch of acerbity.

'In the office?'

'Most of the time. Look, Jennifer love, I'm not in the mood for an inquisition. I'm sorry about this evening . . .'

'Daddy's missing, too.'

'I'm not missing and I'm sure he's not either,' Murray said wearily. 'He's probably trying to call you at this very moment, but can't get through.'

'Would you like me to come back straightaway?'

'No. I'm going to bed and then I'll be fine.'

Jennifer seemed reluctant to replace the receiver even after her husband had rung off and continued to clutch it in her hand as if it were a lifeline.

'Well, at least we know Murray's all right,' her mother remarked when her daughter rejoined her in the drawing-room.

'He sounds anything but all right,' Jennifer said in a worried tone.

'I mean, he's safe at home. But what are we going to do about daddy? He normally always phones if he's held up. Moreover he never mentioned that he was going out and didn't leave a note.' Molly glanced at her watch. 'If he's not back in the next fifteen minutes, I shall call the hospital.'

'Surely they'd have called you if he'd been taken there.'

'He mightn't have been able to speak,' Molly said tremulously.

'But he'd have some means of identification on him. His driving licence and all those credit cards he carries in his wallet.'

'He didn't take his wallet with him,' Molly said. 'It's still in his jacket pocket. He must have gone out in his windcheater, which has no inside pocket.' She gave her daughter an anguished look. 'Where can he have got to?'

Twenty minutes later with all thoughts of food now gone, Molly began a series of telephone calls. First to Grainfield General Hospital which drew a blank, then to the police which was equally unproductive.

'He's probably dropped in on some friends and forgotten the time,' a sergeant said in a calming voice. 'You know what men are!'

118

'It's not like my husband,' Molly protested.

'All husbands fall by the wayside a bit in Christmas week,' the voice asserted confidently. 'As long as he doesn't drive, all will be well.'

Far from reassured, Molly decided to phone a number of friends whom he might conceivably have visited. After the first, however, when she got drawn into a futile conversation about the best sort of stuffing for a Christmas turkey, she asked Jennifer to take over and speak to the others in her list. But none of them had seen Rex that evening, nor could they cast any light upon his whereabouts. One or two asked if there was anything they could do to help, but Jennifer replied in a determinedly bright voice that she was sure he would turn up shortly and was only ringing round in case he had lost count of the time.

Around ten-thirty she tried phoning home, but could get no reply.

'Murray's obviously switched off the bedside phone,' she said in a frustrated tone, 'and our new au pair could sleep through a twenty-one gun salute fired inside her room.'

At midnight Molly called the hospital and the police station again. On this occasion an officer took particulars of Rex and of his car and said he would get those out on night patrol to keep an eye open.

Jennifer offered to stop the night with her mother, but Molly said she'd be all right and was proposing to wrap herself in an eiderdown and stay downstairs on the sofa.

At five o'clock she got up and made herself tea. Thereafter, with no further prospect of sleep, she sat slumped in a state of numbed fear. Eventually dawn brought mist and a grey drizzle. Jennifer called around eight-thirty, but they didn't talk for long.

An hour later the phone rang and a brisk kindly voice asked to speak to Mrs Kline. Molly braced herself for the worst. She knew it could only be bad news.

119

As though on cue, the voice went on, 'I'm afraid I have bad news for you, Mrs Kline. Your husband has been found dead . . . Are you still there, Mrs Kline? Are you all right?'

'Yes, please go on,' she said in a faltering tone. 'What exactly happened to him?'

'His body's been found in a shelter beside the third tee on Grainfield golf course.'

Molly's head swam. She felt like letting out a burst of hysterical laughter and asking what was so special about the third tee? Then she fainted, so that the voice received no reply when it went on a trifle anxiously, 'Are you still all right, Mrs Kline?'

CHAPTER TWENTY-ONE

It was Kenny, the youngest member of the ground staff, who discovered the body. He had gone into the shelter to get out of the rain (not that he ever needed an excuse to hide himself from the head greenkeeper) and to read his newspaper, in particular to make his selections for the afternoon's racing.

His first thought was that a tramp had dossed down there for the night. But why should anyone, even a tramp, sleep on the cement floor when there was a perfectly good wooden bench on which to stretch out? Kenny moved cautiously forward and peered down at the recumbent figure. What he saw caused him to suck in his breath in a noisy gasp and step back with more alacrity than he had shown since he had stepped on a grass snake two summers ago.

At that moment a voice floated through the drizzle outside. 'If I find you in that shelter, Kenny, I'll skin you alive.'

It was followed almost immediately by the threatening figure of the head greenkeeper.

'There's a body in here, Mr Kettleborough,' Kenny said through chattering teeth.

'What are you on about boy?' Arthur Kettleborough was both hard of hearing and short of temper.

'Look, Mr Kettleborough, a body!' Kenny shouted.

'Wake him up then! Our shelter's not a blooming doss house for the homeless.'

'He's dead, Mr Kettleborough.' By this time the head greenkeeper was inside the shelter and staring down at the body.

'He's dead, boy,' he said in an awestruck tone.

'I know. Look at that thing sticking out of his neck. He's been murdered.'

'Somebody's pulled that blooming thing out of the tee,' Arthur Kettleborough said in an affronted tone. 'Run back to the club house and call the police. I'll wait here. Go on, boy, run!'

Without further urging Kenny sped away through the drizzle, while Arthur Kettleborough sat down as far away from the corpse as he could and lit a cigarette to calm his nerves. He found, however, that he was unable to take his eyes off the lifeless shape at the other end of the shelter.

Rex Kline lay face down in a posture that suggested he had first sunk to his knees and then fallen forward. From the right side of his neck protruded a metal arrow sign that Kettleborough recognised as one of those used to indicate the path to a tee. It was the sharp end normally stuck into the ground that had pierced his neck while the arrow itself pointed incongruously toward his feet.

The shelter lay about fifty yards from a side road, but was hidden from view by a small thicket.

It took no more than half an hour for the police to arrive, by which time Kenny had returned breathless, but determined to be on hand.

Detective Chief Inspector Russell had been at the station when the call came through and left immediately accompanied by Detective Inspector Bonham and Detective Constable Parry. The last-named, who was a weekend golfer, professed to know exactly where the shelter was located.

'Who discovered the body?' Russell enquired after casting a quick eye over the scene.

122

'I did, sir,' Kenny said promptly.

'And I was here almost as soon,' Arthur Kettleborough broke in.

'Have either of you touched anything?'

'Not likely,' Kettleborough replied, while Kenny vigorously shook his head.

'Never seen him before in my life,' the head greenkeeper went on as though to ward off an imminent accusation.

'Oh, I know who he is all right,' Russell observed in a weary tone. 'It's Mr Kline.'

'Never 'eard of 'im.'

'He's Mr Riston's father-in-law.'

'Never 'eard of 'im neither.'

'That proves what a blameless life you lead, Mr Kettleborough. Mr Riston is Grainfield's new prosecuting solicitor.'

'Oh!' Arthur Kettleborough stared at the corpse afresh as if this was the least he could do. His expression was one of total bemusement. Russell's was not far removed. Logic told him that there must be a connection between the two murders. But what?

The murderer, whoever he was, had a crude habit of going for his victims' throats. Nothing was going to persuade Russell it was a woman's crime. Once time of death had been established it would be necessary to check Caroline Allard's movements, but he was already sure, more sure than ever, that she couldn't have done it. He realised, however, that Tarr would be far from ready to relinquish his own certainties, which was why he felt so depressed as he stared down at Rex Kline's mortal remains.

He had encountered a fair number of murder victims in the course of his career and, save when they were children, was able to view them dispassionately. On this occasion, however, he neither felt dispassionate, nor was he burning with the fierce anger that the death of a child invoked in him.

123

He just wanted to walk away and leave others to get on with it.

But that impractical course of action was rendered even more so by the arrival of Chief Superintendent Tarr, who took one glance at the body, grunted and, fixing Russell with an impatient look, said, 'O.K., who discovered what and when?'

After Russell's brief recital of events, Tarr took him aside and said, 'As soon as the doctor arrives and gives us some idea of time of death, we'll be on to Caroline Allard. Her reaction to our arrival should be interesting. And the sooner we get there, the more interesting it will be,' he added grimly.

'It doesn't look like a woman's crime to me, sir,' Russell said boldly.

'There's no such thing these days. The woman who used to poison her husband's bedtime cocoa is today as likely as not to fracture his skull with the kitchen hammer.'

It was half an hour before Dr Sinclair arrived, by which time the shelter and its vicinity had been scoured for clues without obvious success. The murderer, with a singular lack of consideration, had failed to shed any buttons or similar tell-tale items at the scene of his crime.

'We found one of her hairs at the previous scene,' Tarr remarked grimly, 'so I want this whole area gone over with a fine toothcomb.'

It seemed to Russell that the murderer and his victim had pre-arranged their meeting-place and that while the murderer had prepared himself, his victim had been unsuspecting. It remained to be seen whether any fingerprints would be found on the arrow that stuck obscenely from Rex Kline's neck.

After a brief examination Dr Sinclair said that, in his estimation, death had occurred over twelve hours previously, but that a more detailed examination of the body would be required to establish it more accurately. It would also be necessary to consider the overnight temperature and the weather conditions.

'Come on,' Tarr said to Russell, 'we're going to visit Miss Allard. She's our number one priority.'

Russell reluctantly followed the Chief Superintendent to his car. The whole investigation had become a nightmare. And Tarr's behaviour more that of a megalomaniac with each passing day.

CHAPTER TWENTY-TWO

'Why don't you come with me?' Rosa said. 'It'll do you good to get out. You can sit in the car or go for a walk while I'm talking to her. Indeed, you could come in with me.'

Caroline shook her head as if the suggestion was completely unacceptable.

'I'll get on with some decorating,' she said.

In the past few days she had been painting the kitchen and bathroom and refusing to leave the cottage even to go shopping, so that this chore now fell to Rosa.

Rosa recognised the need for Caroline to absorb herself in some therapeutic pursuit, but painting the kitchen and bathroom on the eve of Christmas seemed unnecessarily wayward. It made the prospect of roast turkey and a hot bath, in either order, seem questionable.

The only time Rosa could persuade her to leave the cottage was after dark when they would drive to a pub in the neighbourhood where they weren't known and then straight home again after a snack and a quick drink. Even though they never went to the same place twice, Caroline was always on edge and ready to leave. Rosa realised that withdrawal from normal life was a natural reaction to the body blow Caroline had received and was a continuing symptom of the state of shock which had ensued.

'I should be back in a couple of hours,' Rosa said, as she pulled a small woolly cap over her ears. It was dark green with apricot-coloured rings and made her appear more elfin-like than ever.

'I'll be here.'

'And if the phone goes . . .'

'I probably shan't answer it,' Caroline said firmly.

It was yet another sign of her state of withdrawal and one to which she had only confessed the previous day. Rosa had said something about phone calls while she was out and Caroline had said with a shrug, 'I just let it ring when you're not here.'

'It may be my office trying to call me,' Rosa had said reasonably.

'Then they'll try again later if it's important.'

On this occasion Rosa didn't argue, but let herself out of the front door and, head down, ran through the drizzle to where her car was parked at the side of the cottage.

During the five days she had spent with Caroline, she had become conversant with most of the by-roads in the area and had no difficulty finding her way to the house where Mrs Doreen Dingle lived.

Mrs Dingle had been Tom Hunsey's cleaning lady for nearly ten years and Rosa was hoping to learn something useful from her. Mrs Dingle had sounded loquacious on the phone which gave Rosa both hope and an impending sense of resignation.

It took her twenty minutes to reach her destination, a semi-detached built in the familiar and totally unimaginative style of the mid-twenties. As she drew up outside she had a fleeting glimpse of an eager face peering out of a front window. Then it vanished and a lace curtain fell across the gap.

She had barely reached the front door when it opened and the face reappeared.

'Hello, dear. I'm Mrs Dingle. Got lost on the way, did you?'

'No. I'm not late, am I?'

Mrs Dingle let out a laugh. 'I'm a terror for punctuality,' she said. 'Never late all the time I worked for Mr Hunsey. Snow, fog, rain, you name it, dear, I was always there on time. I always say you're either born that way or you're not. Anyway, come in. I've put the kettle on and then you can start asking me your questions.'

Rosa had the impression of being put at her ease before a royal audience. Left alone in the front room she glanced about her. Holiday bric à brac abounded. It was the largest collection she had ever seen except in a shop. Meanwhile from the kitchen came an enthusiastic rendering of Fats Waller's *My very good friend the milkman said*. Rosa wondered if there was anything Freudian in the choice. A couple of minutes later, Mrs Dingle came in bearing a tray. As she put it down Rosa observed that it carried the inscription *Greetings from Bexhill-on-Sea*, while the teapot proclaimed itself *A present from Teignmouth*.

'Milk and sugar, dear?'

'Just milk. No sugar, thank you.'

'Now what is it you wanted to ask me?' Mrs Dingle enquired as she passed Rosa her cup.

'Perhaps I ought to ask you first if you know Miss Allard?'

'Never actually met her, but, of course, I know who you mean.'

'Did Mr Hunsey ever mention her?'

'He may have done, dear. But I only used to see Mr Hunsey on Saturdays when I went in for my money and to give the place an extra bit of polish. Otherwise I had my key and let myself in and out. Mr Hunsey had usually left for work by the time I arrived.'

'What sort of person was he?'

'As nice and kind a gentleman as you could ever hope to meet,' Mrs Dingle said in a wistful tone. 'He had his funny ways, mind you, but who hasn't?'

'What sort of funny ways?' Rosa enquired dutifully.

'He was kind of jumpy in his conversation. And he'd say funny things like, "my poor old aunt was stung by a bee on her eightieth birthday. Take care you don't get stung on your eightieth birthday, Mrs D." Always called me Mrs D, he did. Once he asked me if my husband warmed his feet on me in bed. Things like that; they'd just suddenly come out. But you couldn't mind because he was always such a gentleman.'

Rosa found it difficult to reconcile Tom Hunsey's curious conversational gambits with her own idea of a perfect gentleman, but refrained from comment.

Meanwhile, Mrs Dingle, after sipping her tea, went on, 'He'd get terribly upset if he found an injured bird in the garden. Once there was a dead hedgehog on the lawn and he left a note asking me to bury it as he couldn't bear to go near it. And there was a time a few years ago when he found somebody lying out in the road who'd been knocked down by a car and it took him months to get over the shock of it.'

'Yes, I'd heard about that,' Rosa said. 'I gathered he was in his own car coming along behind.'

'Probably,' Mrs Dingle remarked, as if to dismiss accuracy of that sort as a fad.

'Did he talk to you about it?'

'He was haunted by the poor soul who was killed. Kept on saying how one minute he was alive and well and pedalling home to his wife and the next he was in paradise. "Don't suppose he needs his bike there, Mrs D," he said in his funny way.' Mrs Dingle seemed to become misty-eyed in her reminiscence. 'He used to say he hoped the driver of the car that did it wouldn't have a good night's sleep for the rest of his life because he'd be tormented by his conscience.'

Rosa was thoughtful for a while, then said, 'I suppose the police have interviewed you, Mrs Dingle?'

'I was at Mr Hunsey's house when they searched it. They just asked me a few questions, but that was all.'

'Did you sign a statement?'

She shook her head. 'They said they might want to see me again later. All they were interested in was whether Mr Hunsey ever talked about Miss Allard and if I knew of anything between them. Which I didn't.'

'Do you know if they found anything at his house?'

'They went through all his drawers and took away some of his papers.'

'Did you see what sort of papers?'

'Things from his desk like his bank statements. Old letters. That sort of thing.'

It was just as Rosa would have expected, but they couldn't have found anything that incriminated Caroline, which was obviously what Tarr would have been hoping to find.

'Did Mr Hunsey entertain much?'

'He wasn't one for that,' Mrs Dingle replied as if Rosa had made an unpleasant suggestion. 'Occasionally he'd invite someone in for a meal. Just something simple which he'd prepare himself. He wasn't a fancy eater.'

'Did he ever tell you any of his office gossip?' Rosa enquired.

'Like I told you, dear, I normally only used to see him on Saturdays.' She paused and frowned. 'He certainly never discussed his work with me. To be honest, dear, I'm not interested in all those sordid goings on in court. Never have been.'

'He never talked to you about his colleagues?'

'He might sometimes mention a name, like I said, but generally it was funny things that came suddenly into his head.' A second later she startled Rosa by saying, 'You ever been to Norway, dear?' Rosa shook her head. 'Me and Mr Dingle are thinking of going there on our holidays next summer. We went to Torremolinos last summer, but it was full of foreigners. And I don't go for all that lying on beaches. My skin won't stand it. Now Mr Dingle can lie out in the sun

130

for hours without it bothering him. Anyway, this year we're going to Norway for a change. Mr Dingle says it'll probably rain all the time, but I tell him I'd sooner that than all that oily food you get in Spain.'

'Where will you go, Oslo?'

Mrs Dingle shook her head. 'Not there, somewhere else. I can't remember what it's called. Hang on a minute and I'll get the brochure.' By the time she returned to the room, Rosa was on her feet. 'I can't find it. Mr Dingle must have taken it with him to work to show a friend.' She gave Rosa a surprised look. 'Have you got to go, dear? I was expecting you to ask me lots more questions than you have.'

'If I think of anything else later, I'll call you. You've been a great help, Mrs Dingle, and I'm most grateful.'

'Tell me again what your name is, dear? I'm terrible at remembering them.'

'Rosa Epton.'

'Of course. I shan't forget it now.'

Rosa went out into the hall, where she noticed a garish picture of Torremolinos hanging on one wall and opposite it a silk pennant depicting a sun-drenched Bridlington.

'Goodbye Mrs Dingle,' she said, holding out her hand.

'Goodbye, dear. Just remind me of your name again . . .'

As she drove back to Caroline's cottage, Rosa reflected on her visit. Though it had not produced any blinding revelations, Mrs Dingle had said something which had set off a train of thought; or, rather, given weight to one that was already floating vaguely round her mind.

As she rounded the final bend and Caroline's mist-shrouded cottage came into view, her heart skipped a beat for parked outside was a police car. Its blue roof lamp and its encircling fluorescent stripes gave it the appearance of a bird of particular ill omen.

131

CHAPTER TWENTY-THREE

As Rosa hurried up the path to the front door she could see Caroline staring at her out of the window. Her long, faintly equine face was expressionless and might have been carved in stone. Behind her Rosa could discern the figures of Tarr and Russell standing in the middle of the room. Tarr appeared to be addressing Caroline's back while Russell shifted restlessly beside him.

Rosa burst into the cottage and straight into the living-room without pausing to remove her outdoor clothes. As she did so, Caroline swung round.

'I've refused to say anything until you got back,' she said in a tight, breathless tone. She appeared to have difficulty in getting the words out, but went on, 'Murray Riston's father-in-law has been found murdered on the golf course and the police immediately made for here.'

'I've asked Miss Allard to account for her movements between six o'clock and ten o'clock yesterday evening,' Tarr said in a determined voice.

'We were in the whole of yesterday evening,' Rosa remarked.

'I'd prefer Miss Allard to answer for herself.'

'I didn't go out at all yesterday evening,' Caroline said. 'Miss Epton can prove it. We spent the evening here together.'

'Have you any independent proof of that?'

'I've just said, Miss Epton's my witness.'

'I said *independent* proof. Miss Epton hardly falls into that category.'

Rosa flushed. 'I'm not used to being called a liar, even by implication,' she said angrily.

Tarr gave her a wintry smile.

'I'm sure there've been numerous occasions in court when you've suggested that a corroborating police witness is not truly independent. I'd hardly expect you to tell me if Miss Allard did go out between six and ten last night. After all, you're her friend as well as her solicitor. Each role as inhibiting as the other in the present circumstances.' He turned to Caroline. 'Did you go out at all yesterday?'

She shook her head. 'No. I did some gardening in the morning and got on with painting the bathroom in the afternoon when it began to rain.'

'Was Miss Epton with you the whole day?'

Caroline gave Rosa a helpless look. 'No, she went up to London to attend to business in her office. She arrived back between six and seven.'

'Can't you be more precise than that?'

'I'd say between six and half past. I was watching Nationwide on BBC 1 when she returned.'

'And neither of you went out again?'

'That's correct.'

'How did you spend the evening?'

'I continued painting and Miss Epton got on with some work she'd brought back with her.'

'Did you have any visitors?'

'No.'

'Phone calls?'

'I think there were a couple. Miss Epton took them.'

'Would you care to tell me, Miss Epton, who called?'

'Mrs Shoreham was one,' Rosa said in a suddenly embarrassed tone.

'Who did she want to speak to?' Tarr asked with quickening interest.

'Miss Allard. But I told her she was up a ladder and covered in paint and couldn't come to the phone.'

'Or was the truth, Miss Allard, that you weren't at home at all?'

'I was certainly at home.'

'Why couldn't you have spoken to Mrs Shoreham?'

'Miss Epton's explained.'

'And the second call?'

Caroline and Rosa exchanged a further glance.

'The second call was from the rector,' Rosa said. 'He wanted to know if Miss Allard would like him to visit her.'

'And?'

'I said I'd ask her to call him back.'

'What reason did you give *him* for not fetching Miss Allard to the phone?' Tarr enquired in a biting tone.

Rosa reacted as if he had jabbed a needle into her.

'Let's be quite clear where we stand, Mr Tarr. If I go on answering your questions, it's out of courtesy and not out of any sense of duty toward the police.'

'But also out of a desire to help Miss Allard, I'm sure.'

'Of course.'

'So what excuse did you give the rector?'

'The same as I gave Mrs Shoreham.'

'So what it amounts to is this: Miss Allard says she spent the evening at home and you support her in that. On two occasions you answer the phone and tell the caller that Miss Allard is up a ladder and covered in paint and can't be disturbed.' He paused. 'Surely you must see, Miss Epton, that independent corroboration of her presence at home the whole evening is very desirable from a police point of view, as well as being very much in Miss Allard's own interest? I stress the word independent.'

'I do not tell lies on behalf of my clients,' Rosa said

134

disdainfully.

'What about on behalf of your friends?' Tarr enquired with a small superior smile. 'I'm sure you'd lie to help a friend. Most of us do at one time or another. It's natural.' The smile became quietly triumphant.

Rosa felt embarrassed, not because she considered she had been caught out, but because Caroline's refusal to have visitors and even to answer the phone had placed her in a false position. Tarr had sensed an immediate undercurrent between the two women and had assumed that Rosa was lying as a cover-up. It would be hopeless to try and explain the truth to him, namely that Caroline had been in a particularly jittery mood the previous evening and had flatly refused to speak to anyone on the phone.

'I should like to take a quick look at your car, Miss Allard,' Tarr went on.

She gave a nod and then looked helplessly at Rosa.

'I'll go with him,' Rosa said.

Followed by the two officers, she led the way to the garage and watched them examine Caroline's Renault. Tarr bent down and inspected the tyres while Russell opened the driver's door and took a note of the milometer reading. Rosa could well understand Tarr's interest in the tyres, for like the soles of shoes and the turn-ups on trousers they might be able to provide a range of significant clues. As far as Rosa could see, however, they bore no obvious tell-tale marks as to where the car had been driven.

'When did Miss Allard last go out in her car?' Tarr asked in a seemingly casual tone.

'Not since you arrested her. When we've been out together, we've always gone in my car.'

'But for all you know she may have gone out yesterday while you were away in London?'

'She told me she'd not been out all day,' Rosa said firmly. 'And she certainly didn't leave the house after my return.'

'So you've told me,' Tarr remarked drily. After a thoughtful pause, he went on, 'You'll appreciate, Miss Epton, that we're still in the early stages of investigating Mr Kline's death and that I shall need to talk to Miss Allard again when the experts have reported on their findings at the scene. As you'll be aware, they descend like particularly determined vultures.' He gave Rosa a thin smile. 'I shall be sending one of the vultures to examine Miss Allard's car so perhaps you'd ensure she doesn't use it until he has done so. Mr Russell has taken the milometer reading so we'll know if it is taken out on the road before then. No need for us to come back into the house, so I'll leave you to tell Miss Allard the position.'

As Rosa watched them drive off she decided their visit had been nothing other than an exercise in intimidation. They had hoped Caroline would break down and confess. They obviously didn't have sufficient evidence to take the case against her any farther, but had nevertheless been unwilling to wait until the so-called vultures had visited the scene. Rosa accepted it was a reasonable assumption that the same person had killed both Tom Hunsey and Rex Kline. That person was definitely not Caroline and only Chief Superintendent Tarr seemed to think otherwise. Rosa had seldom seen an officer looking as ill at ease and uncomfortable as Detective Chief Inspector Russell.

She turned to go back into the cottage. She hadn't yet had a chance to tell Caroline about her visit to Mrs Dingle. She was also eager to try out her theory of Tom Hunsey's murder. Admittedly it was a theory with gaps, not least of which was the actual identity of the murderer. Nevertheless it was going to take more than a tepid reaction from Caroline to put her off, especially as she now saw Rex Kline's murder as filling one of the gaps.

CHAPTER TWENTY-FOUR

Never the most cheerful of buildings, Grainfield Manor grew more gloomy by the day. Its occupants found themselves talking in furtive whispers and then only out of professional necessity. Each in his own way looked forward to Christmas, not so much for its festivities as an opportunity to get away from the oppressive atmosphere for a few days.

Work went on, people prepared their cases and appeared in court, but that was about all. They performed like so many soloists without a conductor.

On the day his father-in-law was found murdered Murray Riston called his secretary around ten o'clock to say he would not be coming in. He offered no explanation over the phone, but when she went dutifully to inform Charles Buck, he nodded and said, 'I didn't expect to see him today. You've heard, of course?'

'Heard what, Mr Buck?'

'That Mr Kline, his father-in-law, has been found murdered.'

Miss Vincent went pale. 'Oh, how terrible! What on earth's happening to us? There's been nothing but tragedy since Mr Patching left.'

'And there could be more to come.'

Miss Vincent recoiled. 'Don't say things like that, Mr Buck!'

'No point in not facing up to reality. There's a murderer in

137

our midst and until he's been brought to book, one can't be certain of anything.'

She gave him a sharp look. 'You're not referring to Miss Allard, I take it?' she said with a boldness that surprised her.

'Chief Superintendent Tarr seems to believe she's guilty . . .' His internal phone gave an imperious buzz and he lifted the receiver. After listening for a few seconds, he said, 'Very well, I'll see him as soon as he arrives.' Glancing up at Miss Vincent he remarked, 'Talk of the devil, Mr Tarr's on his way here now. If Mr Riston calls again you can assure him that the building hasn't collapsed and that everyone is at work despite his absence.'

Miss Vincent turned on her heel and departed, leaving the deputy C.P.S. to await Tarr's arrival.

'Sorry I'm late,' Tarr said briskly striding into the room some forty-five minutes later. 'I got held up. I gather the C.P.S. isn't in today.'

'That's hardly surprising.'

'How are you adjusting to the new regime?'

Buck shrugged. 'There won't be much left of any regime unless you make an arrest shortly,' he said with a mirthless smile.

'I haven't come here to spar with you,' Tarr said severely. 'Tell me where you were between six and ten yesterday evening? Nothing personal you understand. All part of the routine.'

'I was at home with my wife,' Buck said in an unamused tone.

'Just the two of you?'

'Yes.'

'Of course you live quite close to the golf course, do you not?'

'I do.' His tone seemed to defy Tarr to make anything of the admission.

'Well that seems to be that then,' Tarr remarked.

Buck looked at him in surprise. 'Is that all you came to ask me?'

'As a matter of fact there was one other matter. I understand you moved the weapon with which Hunsey was killed from the doorman's desk and hid it behind a curtain. Is that correct?'

Buck stared at his interrogator with a wary expression.

'May I ask who told you that?'

'You know I can't divulge my sources of information. But is it true?'

'Yes, it is,' he said after a considerable pause. 'I moved it out of sight in case someone was tempted to take it.'

'Steal it, do you mean?'

'Precisely. I thought maybe somebody who'd had a bit too much to drink might be light-fingered on his way out. It's just the sort of thing that might be nicked. I suppose the person who saw me might well be the person who later removed it to commit the murder. I'm sure that must have occurred to you?'

Tarr gazed back dispassionately. With so much ill feeling around in the upper echelons of the C.P.S.'s office, his job should be that much easier. It was when you were up against closed ranks that enquiries became a test of patience and endurance. And yet it wasn't working out that way. In particular the feuding between the C.P.S. and his deputy was, he felt, more of a distraction than anything else.

The fact remained that ever since Hunsey's murder Tarr had felt himself under a strong compulsion to return, and return again, to Grainfield Manor. The place haunted him as much as he had begun to haunt it. He was sure that the clue to the murder would be found there and he believed that his frequent appearances were part of the necessary psychological pressure on its occupants.

On the morning of the discovery of Rex Kline's body he had found himself once more drawn back there. Thus after

139

the visit to Caroline Allard he had told Russell of his intention, leaving the D.C.I. and his minions to go and interview Molly Kline and the Ristons and generally get on with the second murder enquiry.

With only a few days to go before Caroline reported to Grainfield police station under the terms of her bail, his determination to find some conclusive bit of evidence became even greater. If he was obliged to release her from her bail it would amount to a defeat. And more than a defeat, a humiliation which he refused to contemplate. He had stuck his neck out by taking her into custody and by using the provisions of Section 43 of the Magistrates Courts Act in a highly unorthodox way and he was determined not to be forced into climbing down. He felt that his career was at stake.

It was in this sombre mood that he arrived at the C.P.S.'s headquarters that morning. He knew that the word went round as soon as he set foot inside the building and he hoped that news of the second murder would, so to speak, have softened up the opposition.

After leaving Charles Buck's office he made his way down the main staircase into the hall.

'Hello, sir,' Alec said in a tone of surprise. 'Came in the back way, did you?'

'No. There was nobody here and I just walked in.'

'I only slipped away for a couple of seconds,' Alec said in an aggrieved tone. 'I was taken short and couldn't wait.'

'Let's hope no murderers seized the opportunity of getting in while you were absent,' Tarr remarked sardonically.

'Don't say things like that, sir! You won't tell anyone, will you? I don't know what Mr Buck would do if he found out. He'd really tear me off a strip.'

'If I don't tell on you, what are you going to do for me in return?'

Alec smiled hopefully, as if he had gained a reprieve.

'I've been keeping my ears open like you asked me,' he said. 'But it's as though people are afraid to talk. Everyone seems scared.'

'You must have picked up something,' Tarr pressed him.

'I might be telling you what you already know,' he said in a suddenly prevaricating tone.

'Try me.'

'I did hear about something Mr Shoreham's supposed to have heard,' Alec said, carefully observing Tarr's reaction to this enigmatic utterance.

'Go on, I'm interested.'

'He heard Miss Allard's door being shut just before poor Mr Hunsey was discovered dead.'

'The door of her office?'

'Yes.'

'When did you learn this?'

'Only yesterday.'

'Who told you?'

'Well, it's like this. My wife has a friend, Madge, who works for Mrs Shoreham and she happened to hear Mr Shoreham telling Mrs Shoreham how he was sure he'd heard Miss Allard's door being closed just before George Ives came and told him how he'd found the body. Mrs Shoreham asked him if he'd told the police and he said he hadn't.'

Tarr gave a thoughtful nod. 'What's Madge's other name?'

'Mrs Owen.'

'Her address?'

'She lives next to us in Totland Road. Number 14.'

'Did she overhear any further conversation between Mr and Mrs Shoreham?'

'That was all she told my wife. You could ask her yourself.'

'I shall. Is Mr Shoreham in this morning?'

'He's in court.'

141

'Which court?'

Alec consulted a typed list on his desk.

'West Burland. He should be back after lunch. Hold on a minute, that's his car just gone past.'

A couple of minutes later, Peter Shoreham came in through the front door. He gave Tarr a brief nod.

'A wasted journey,' he observed. 'Defendant failed to turn up. What an imperfect system we operate!'

'I wonder if I might have a word with you, Mr Shoreham,' Tarr said.

'Here? Or do you want to come up to my room?'

'It'd be better in your room,' Tarr replied firmly.

'Have a chair,' Peter said as he closed his door behind them. He tossed his briefcase down beside his desk and turned to face Tarr. 'What can I do for you?'

Though he affected to speak casually, his voice betrayed his nervousness.

'You can give a truthful answer to a simple question,' Tarr said.

'As long as you don't expect a lawyer to answer any question yes or no,' Peter remarked with a forced smile. 'That's what they expect from witnesses, not from each other.'

'This question can easily be answered yes or no,' Tarr said without a smile. 'On the evening of the party did you hear Miss Allard's door being closed shortly before you accompanied George Ives outside?'

Peter paled, then assumed a heavy frown.

'What an odd question,' he said uncomfortably.

'Yes or no, Mr Shoreham?'

'Why should I be expected to remember something as insignificant as a door closing?'

'Because you obviously didn't regard it as insignificant. And neither do I, if it's true.'

Peter was silent and sat staring with a drawn expression

142

across the room. Eventually he said in a tight voice, 'Since you ask, I did hear a door close about the time you mention. Or rather I thought I did. But I could easily have been mistaken.'

'Was it Miss Allard's door?'

'I really couldn't say. It might have been any of several.'

'Where were you at the time?'

'At the top of the stairs.'

'And the sound came from where?'

'It was difficult to say.'

'This is a serious matter, Mr Shoreham,' Tarr said severely. 'The fact that you never mentioned it when you were interviewed is serious enough, your present evasiveness makes it that much worse. I wouldn't want to think you're actually trying to obstruct me in my enquiries.'

'That's absolute rubbish!'

'I'm not so sure. I think you should consider your position very carefully. Miss Allard's room is the only one situated on that particular half-landing. If the sound came from that direction, it could only have been her door. Moreover, it's clear to me that you believed it was her door.'

Peter put his head in his hands and let out a groan.

'I still can't say for certain,' he said miserably.

'But you were certain enough in your own mind, weren't you?'

'I jumped to a conclusion, something a lawyer should never do.'

'This has nothing to do with being a lawyer. And now I'd like to take a short statement from you dealing with the point.'

'I'll write one out and let you have it.'

'All right, but I'm waiting here while you do so. I don't want any reneging.' Peter seemed about to protest, but Tarr went on, 'Just remember what I said about obstructing the police, Mr Shoreham, because I meant it.' He opened his document case. 'Here's an official statement form which you can use.'

With a defeated air Peter took it and began to write.

After leaving Peter Shoreham's room, Tarr made his way to Caroline Allard's where he spent several minutes opening and closing the door. While he was doing so, a C.I.D. officer from headquarters came round the corner and Tarr called out to him.

'Just open and close this door a few times while I go and listen at the top of the stairs.'

'Slam it, do you mean, sir?'

'No, I don't mean. Do it quietly as if you didn't want anybody to hear.'

Tarr moved away and positioned himself where he assumed Peter Shoreham had stood. A few seconds later the sound of several unmistakable clicks reached his ears. As unmistakable as the sound itself was the direction from which it came.

He returned to where the officer was still dutifully opening and closing the door.

'O.K., you can stop now. Do you agree it's impossible to shut the door without that final click?'

'Absolutely, sir.'

Tarr gave a satisfied nod. 'We may need to call you as an expert witness on door closing,' he observed jocularly.

'How's the investigation going, sir?'

'One could say a bit better within the past half hour,' Tarr remarked as he walked away.

On the spur of the moment, he decided to go and take a look at Tom Hunsey's room. He had had it searched during the early stages of the enquiry, but it had failed to reveal any clues. He was still certain, however, that somewhere within the walls of Grainfield Manor lay the answers to many unresolved questions. The events of the morning had helped to sustain his belief.

Hunsey's room was reached by a short spiral staircase that led nowhere else. It was hexagonal in shape and from without gave the impression of an excrescence that bulged outwards between two right angle walls. It had been unoccupied since the murder and had a musty smell. It was clear that the cleaners had left it well alone for there was a thick film of dust covering both the desk and a small side table on which were a number of legal text books.

'I bet they gathered dust even when he was here,' Tarr muttered to himself as he went across to the window and looked out.

It was as he turned away that the mirror caught his attention. Not so much the mirror itself, for he was already aware of its presence on the wall, as its curious angle. It was held out from the wall at one bottom corner by a wad of folded paper. The effect was that you could stand in a recess beside the window and see reflected in the mirror the interior of another room, Caroline Allard's room half a floor below.

Tarr hummed quietly to himself to celebrate his discovery. After experimenting a while, it became quite clear that Hunsey had provided himself with a perfect view into Caroline Allard's room without being observed.

The wad of paper indicated that it was only used when Hunsey decided he wanted to play peeping tom. Afterwards it was presumably removed and the mirror restored to its natural and untilted position.

So what had Hunsey seen that necessitated Caroline Allard murdering him? For Tarr now had no doubt that he was on his way to discovering the elusive motive.

Tarr descended the winding stairway from Hunsey's room and walked down the short corridor that led to Caroline Allard's. He sat down at her desk and stared out of the window at the hexagonal excrescence which housed the room

145

he had just left. He could see the mirror hanging on the wall to the right of the window. From where he sat it looked innocuous and would arouse nobody's suspicions. He would need to get one of the photographers from headquarters to take a series of pictures illustrating the use to which the mirror could be, and undoubtedly had been, put.

He reached for Caroline's desk diary and began turning the pages. He had done so once before without any particular enlightenment, but now he looked at each entry with fresh interest. It was a record of her official life with reference to court fixtures and conferences with police officers and others.

The entries were meticulously explicit e.g. *R. v. Jones (RTA) Grainfield M.C. 2.30 p.m.* RTA clearly denoted that it was a case under the Road Traffic Act and M.C. stood for Magistrates Court. Conferences usually appeared as, for example, *10.30 Det Sgt Grover re Ashley and others*.

It was an entry for Friday, 26th October that caused him to pause and think. It read, *R.v. Manley and others (drugs), Grainfield Crown Court, 10 a.m.* It was a case, he recalled, which had ended in heavy prison sentences on three defendants who had been caught handling cocaine. Two of them had brought it into the country concealed in a spare tyre in their car and were in the process of passing it to the third man when the police, who had received a tip-off, pounced. It had been an open and shut case, but Tarr now recalled there had been a suggestion later that some of the drug was unaccounted for. The officer in charge of the case had been the subject of a disciplinary enquiry which had left the matter unresolved. Hotly proclaiming his innocence he had been exonerated, but the fact remained that a small amount of the cocaine was missing. It had been in small packets like tea bags. There had been several hundred of them so that nobody was likely to notice until they were counted if one or two were missing.

Now supposing Caroline Allard was the actual culprit . . .
She would certainly have had the opportunity . . . Could
this be what Tom Hunsey had got on to?

As Tarr slipped the desk diary into his document case, he
decided it was the most profitable morning he had spent
since the investigation started. It had given him an impetus
which mustn't be allowed to seep away.

Two days before Christmas Caroline and Rosa set out for
Grainfield police station, it being the appointed day for
Caroline to report in accordance with her bail.

A pale sun shone from a lemon-tinged sky and Caroline
peered at it through the car window with the air of one who
was looking at it for the last time.

'I'll tell Detective Chief Inspector Russell you're here,' the
uniformed sergeant said when Rosa announced their
presence at the enquiries desk.

A few minutes later a young plain clothes officer appeared
to escort them up to the C.I.D.

Russell and Tarr both rose when Caroline and Rosa
entered Russell's room. Tarr wore a grim expression while
Russell looked as nervous as on the previous occasion they
had gathered in his room. He motioned the women to be
seated.

'You know why you're here, Miss Allard,' he said in a tone
that was half way between question and statement. Before
anyone could say anything he hurried on, 'But first it's only
fair to give you an opportunity of explaining one or two
matters that have come to light since you were bailed.'

'I take it my client is still under caution?' Rosa broke in.

'Yes.'

'Then she'll neither wish to answer any questions nor offer
any explanations.'

'Is that correct, Miss Allard?' Russell enquired in a
worried voice.

147

'Yes,' Caroline said tensely.

Russell glanced anxiously at Tarr who gave him a nod. Rosa was to reflect afterwards that it was the nod of a tyrant consigning someone to execution.

'Then I must now tell you, Miss Allard,' Russell went on, 'that you will be charged with the murder of Thomas Hunsey on the 2nd of December this year.'

CHAPTER TWENTY-FIVE

Caroline spent Christmas in prison and Rosa couldn't have felt worse if she had been there, too. She had been shattered by the decision to charge Caroline.

The next day, Christmas Eve, Caroline had made a formal appearance before Grainfield Magistrates Court and, despite a passionate plea for bail by Rosa, had been remanded in custody for seven days.

Rosa left court feeling bruised and outraged. The police, in the shape of Detective Chief Inspector Russell, had opposed bail for what Rosa regarded as the usual stale old reasons they trotted out on such occasions. The seriousness of the charge, the possibility of interference with witnesses (she could detect Tarr's hand in that one) and the infamous hint that Caroline might be tempted to take her own life if granted her freedom.

'At least, as I understand it, you're not suggesting she might abscond?' Rosa had said bitterly.

'No, I don't think she would,' Russell had replied fairly.

Afterwards Rosa had spent the unhappiest half hour of her life with Caroline before she was driven off to prison. For most of the time Caroline just sat and stared across the cell in a silent withdrawal from life.

'I'll brief Counsel immediately and get them to apply for bail to a judge in chambers,' she had said.

'You'll be lucky to find anyone around over the holiday,'

149

Caroline had been stirred to remark.

'I'll find somebody all right. I'll get the vacation judge out of bed if necessary.' She had proceeded to mention the names of various counsel, but Caroline showed no interest.

Immediately she left the court she drove back to Caroline's cottage and packed her things. Twenty minutes later she locked up and departed for London. It was a miserable drive with Rosa filled with self-reproach. She felt she had advised Caroline poorly and had been wrong to oppose the police quite so bluntly. She had just never seriously believed Caroline was in danger of being charged . . .

By Christmas evening, after a great many telephone calls, she had secured the services of Martin Ainsworth QC and Paul Elson, a team she had briefed on a number of occasions.

Ainsworth was a bachelor and had a flat in Knightsbridge. It transpired that he was spending Christmas in London prior to two weeks ski-ing in Switzerland at the beginning of January. He had a soft spot for Rosa as a person and a considerable respect for her professional ability. When she said in her relief that he could go away for as long as he wanted in January provided he got Caroline out on bail, he laughed and said he'd have a good try.

Paul Elson she ran to earth at his home in Kent. He was a tubby, perennially cheerful person in his late thirties whose breezy manner belied an extremely astute mind.

'Good gracious, Rosa!' he exclaimed when he heard her voice on the line. 'Don't you ever take a break? Nip into your car and drive down here for a spot of turkey and pud. I mean it.'

She could hear children's excited voices in the background and could picture Paul wearing a funny hat as they talked. When she told him the reason for her call, his response had been immediate.

'Of course, Rosa. Just let me know time and place and I'll be there. I'm supposed to be taking ten days off, but a visit to the vacation judge is always an adventure.'

Three days later Rosa and her two counsel, plus one representing the police, foregathered at the home of Mr Justice Annerly, who lived in a large house on the edge of Hampstead Heath. In the splendour of his oak-panelled study he listened attentively to Martin Ainsworth's plea and to the objections to bail advanced on behalf of the police.

When they had finished, he said with a pleasant lack of fuss, 'I am prepared to grant the defendant bail in the wholly exceptional circumstances of this case.' Rising from his desk he added amiably, 'And now let's all get back to our Christmas pleasures!'

After expressing her gratitude to her two counsel, Rosa drove home almost light-headed with relief. For the moment she was unwilling to let her mind dwell on the formidable task ahead.

Later that day she met a bemused Caroline on her release from prison.

CHAPTER TWENTY-SIX

In due course Caroline's trial was fixed to start on Monday, April 14th at Grainfield Crown Court, where the presiding judge was scheduled to be Mr Justice Farrow.

She had been committed for trial by the Grainfield magistrates at the beginning of February. After consultation with counsel it had been decided that the defence should accept a 'paper' committal and should not require the attendance of any of the prosecution's witnesses at that stage, all of whose statements had been served on the defence. In the result the committal for trial was no more than a two minute formality, the only drama coming when Russell, at Tarr's instigation, suggested to the court that the question of revoking bail ought to be considered in view of the change of circumstances. Fortunately the court gave short shrift to what was, at best, a half-hearted application and Russell was left to face a fuming chief superintendent, who wished he had brushed protocol aside and dealt with the matter himself.

For Rosa, January and February were the busiest months she could remember. In between attending to her normal load of work, she made frequent trips to Grainfield, some heralded, many not, in order to pursue her own enquiries. Caroline had agreed to go and stay with an aunt in Bath where, as a condition of her bail, she reported to the police once a week. A further condition had been that she should surrender her passport. Rosa kept in frequent touch with her by telephone and also paid her a number of visits to discuss details of her defence.

By the end of February Rosa, following some deep burrowing into the past, thought she knew who had committed the murder and why. If she was right, it followed that the same person had also murdered Rex Kline. Even Caroline in her chronic state of depression was moved to show interest when Rosa propounded her theory.

At the beginning of March she delivered her briefs to counsel and asked for a consultation at their earliest convenience to discuss defence strategy. She mentioned that she wished Caroline to be present.

On the day the briefs reached counsel she phoned each of their clerks and stressed the importance of not leaving the papers out where prying eyes might see them.

A few days later Martin Ainsworth's clerk got in touch with her and suggested 4 o'clock on a Wednesday two weeks hence for the consultation.

Caroline came up from Bath by train that morning and Rosa met her at Paddington and took her out to lunch. Afterwards they went to an exhibition at the Tate and just before four that afternoon arrived at Martin Ainsworth's chambers in Mulberry Court in the Temple. Paul Elson had arrived ahead of them and was closeted with his leader. Robert, the chambers' senior clerk, greeted Rosa rather as a floor manager might welcome a very special customer to his department. Caroline was impressed and secretly amused. She knew a large number of barristers' clerks, but had never received such pampered treatment herself.

When she murmured as much to Rosa as they waited to be shown into Martin Ainsworth's room, Rosa said, 'It's not me, it's you. Like it or not, you're a *cause célèbre* in the making.'

Caroline grimaced. It hadn't occurred to her and the thought was distinctly unappealing. She had never met either of her counsel in the course of her own professional life, but knew of Ainsworth's reputation as a much sought after

153

defence advocate.

'Mr Ainsworth's ready now,' Robert said, suddenly reappearing in front of them.

As they entered his spacious room, with its large bay window looking out on Mulberry Court, Elson jumped to his feet beaming like a schoolboy who had just been given an unexpected £5 note. Martin Ainsworth came round his desk to shake hands. He was of medium height and looked as fit now as when he had played tennis for Oxford thirty years ago. His skin glowed with a healthy tan, his eyes were alert and his hair, which was light brown, bore only a few traces of grey.

'I suggest you take that chair, Miss Allard,' he said, after Rosa had made the introductions. 'I happen to know Rosa hates it.'

'It swallows me up,' Rosa said with a smile. 'And it's hopeless if you're trying to sort through papers,' she added as she opened her briefcase and pulled out a bulging file.

Paul Elson, meanwhile, had slipped the length of pink tape off his brief and was carefully unknotting it as he waited for his leader to open the proceedings.

Fixing his gaze on Caroline, Martin Ainsworth said, 'I think this is one of the most remarkable cases in which I've ever been asked to defend. Remarkable for three reasons; the first being the extraordinary conduct of Chief Superintendent Tarr and the second being a lawyer charged with the murder of another lawyer, both members of a prosecuting solicitor's staff.' He paused and added in a tentative voice, 'I'm sure it must even strike you as bizarre, Miss Allard.'

'To me it's a continuing nightmare,' Caroline said with a grimace.

'Of course it must be and I didn't mean to cause you any offence by my comment.'

'That's all right. Seen objectively I suppose it must appear bizarre. My trouble is I'm unable to see it objectively.'

'And the third reason?' Rosa broke in.

154

'The third reason,' Ainsworth went on, switching his attention to her, 'is that, for the first time in my career, I'm being instructed to play the role of Perry Mason. I'm not to be content with securing my client's acquittal, but I'm to demonstrate to the court who actually did commit the murder.' He drew a deep breath and blew out his cheeks. 'Isn't that going a bit far? In my view Miss Allard has an excellent chance of being acquitted on the evidence as it stands – and I don't often say that to my lay clients – so why do you wish to make things more difficult than they need be, Rosa? Do we really want Perry Mason prowling round Grainfield Crown Court?'

Rosa brushed back her hair that had fallen across her face as she leaned forward to listen to counsel.

'You don't accept my theory of the crime?' she said.

'I think you've done a superb investigative job,' Ainsworth said quickly. 'All I'm saying is that it's not necessary in defending Miss Allard to point an accusing finger at anyone else. I think you should pass the results of your own enquiries to the police.'

'When?'

'When?' Ainsworth echoed warily.

Rosa nodded. 'Obviously not before the trial because they'd ignore it. Afterwards? If Caroline's acquitted, they'll still believe she did it and won't be interested in re-opening their file. Should she be convicted, there'd be even less chance of their taking any action. It would need a national campaign to get them to do anything and we all know the odds one is up against there.

'I'm convinced I'm right, but I'm the first to agree that I've not built up a strong case evidentially; there's too much speculation and not enough solid proof. But all that could be put right by a confrontation in court. Moreover, it *is* an essential part of the defence. It must be. If you can demonstrate who did murder Tom Hunsey, it absolves

Caroline more surely than anything else.'

'She's right about that, Martin,' Paul Elson said. Then in a peace-making tone he went on, 'But we don't have to take a decision today. Indeed, my own view is that it'll be a matter of playing it by ear. It mayn't become necessary for you to emulate Perry Mason; on the other hand if the need is there I'd put my money on you to outdo him.'

'I'm not sure if that's a compliment or not,' Ainsworth remarked drily. 'Anyway, I agree we don't have to decide the issue now and I know Rosa realises that the conduct of the defence in court has to be counsel's absolute responsibility.'

Rosa nodded. 'Are we also all agreed that the failure of the police to charge anyone in respect of Rex Kline's murder is a major weakness in the prosecution's case? It's so obvious that both murders were committed by one person and Tarr wouldn't have hesitated to charge Caroline if he'd found one jot of evidence to implicate her.'

'I imagine that any questions to the police about Kline's murder will bring forth the answer that it's still under investigation and that there's no evidence of any connection between the two crimes.'

'Which is ridiculous.'

'Don't worry, I shall do what I can to exploit the situation.'

'It stands out a mile that the two murders are connected,' Rosa said indignantly.

'But one can hardly expect the prosecution to accept that lying down. When I bumped into Berry Winskip the other day, he mentioned the case and went out of his way to tell me quite bluntly that so far as he was concerned Kline's murder was irrelevant to our trial.'

Beresford Winskip Q.C. was leading for the prosecution. He belonged to an old school of advocacy who didn't believe in soft approaches or velvet gloves whether he was prosecuting or defending. Rosa knew him only by reputation, but Caroline, who had heard him in action on various occasions, had distinctly mixed feelings about his prosecuting her.

'But the judge can't properly exclude evidence of Rex Kline's murder,' Rosa said with a frown.

'I hope he won't even try, but, as always, it'll be a question of how far he regards it as relevant to the issue before the jury.' Ainsworth gave a reflective smile. 'But crossing swords with Berry Winskip is an occupational hazard at the Bar.'

For the next hour Ainsworth went through the prosecution's evidence, clarifying various points with Caroline and questioning her about the lies she had told the police concerning her movements on the evening of the party and the scratch on her hand.

'Nobody will realise better than you, Miss Allard, how unfortunate it was that you took that course. But the best thing to do now is grasp the nettle firmly and come clean. It will be up to me to persuade the jury that your conduct was understandable and perfectly plausible in the circumstances. I'll come down to Grainfield the evening before the trial and I'd like us all to meet then and have a final word before we go into court.' He glanced toward Elson. 'Anything you want to add, Paul?'

Junior counsel shook his head. 'Only that I wouldn't want to be in Chief Superintendent Tarr's shoes when the whole thing's over. They'll have to transfer him somewhere.'

'There's a special limbo for senior police officers who fall from grace,' Ainsworth observed wryly. 'What about you, Miss Allard, is there anything you want to say before the party breaks up?'

'Only that I'm very grateful to Rosa and to you and Mr Elson,' she said quietly.

'Rosa's certainly done an incredible job,' Ainsworth said. 'Now there's your Perry Mason!'

Rosa laughed. 'And do you really accept my theory about the murders?' she asked.

'Why not?' he said with a conspiratorial wink.

CHAPTER TWENTY-SEVEN

On the Friday before the trial was due to open Rosa went down to Bath by car, picked up Caroline and together they drove to Grainfield. They stopped on their way to buy provisions as Caroline flatly refused to go into any of the local shops where she was known.

The next day they drove to a town about ten miles west of Grainfield in order that she might have her hair done.

'You've got to look your best,' Rosa said firmly.

Caroline was wont to wear her hair pulled straight back and tied in a short pony tail, but Rosa was insistent that it needed a softer and more feminine look.

That same day Rosa went through Caroline's wardrobe to find the right dress for the occasion.

'Anyone would think I'm going to a party,' Caroline remarked as she watched Rosa take out dresses and put them back again.

'In a sense you are. The most important one of your life.'

'All right, I know, it's not every day I get tried for murder.'

Rosa made no comment, but continued looking for a suitable dress.

'What I'm after is something sober, yet fresh and springlike. Certainly nothing you'd wear to court as an advocate. What about this?'

'This' was a dress in a soft shade of pale green with white

trimmings.

'I'll look like a seductress.'

'It's very nice. Besides, seductresses don't wear dresses with such a high neckline and with three quarter length sleeves. It has a lovely mint fresh look about it. Linen, too. Just the job.'

'The defendant looked radiant in pale green with non-matching accessories and her gardening shoes,' Caroline said with a slight giggle.

Rosa let out a laugh and suddenly the tension was broken.

They had arrived at the cottage to find a stack of mail awaiting Caroline. Amongst it were two cards wishing her all the best in her ordeal. One was from Peter and Kay Shoreham, the other from Murray Riston.

'Tarr would have apoplexy if he knew some of his witnesses had sent the equivalent of get-well-cards to the defendant,' Caroline observed.

'It's a nice gesture. I happen to know how badly Peter Shoreham feels about being dragged into the case.'

'And Murray?' Caroline said sardonically.

'Murray Riston's a hypocrite,' Rosa remarked and felt like adding, 'and deserves everything that's coming to him.'

On Sunday evening they drove to the hotel where Martin Ainsworth and Paul Elson were staying. Ainsworth had invited them all to dine with him and had thoughtfully arranged a private room in order to spare Caroline from the inquisitive glances of other guests.

Under the influence of two gins before dinner Caroline became noticeably relaxed. Three glasses of wine during the meal and a liqueur afterwards helped to sustain the process.

'The defendant appeared in court with a hangover by courtesy of her counsel,' she murmured in a slurred voice as she tripped over the door mat on arrival home.

'You'll feel fine in the morning,' Rosa said.

'I'm drunk, Rosa. And I feel terrible.'

159

Twenty minutes later she was in bed and asleep. Rosa left a glass of water on her bedside table before retiring to her own room.

It had been a good evening, not merely socially but professionally as well. She was now confident that Martin Ainsworth was ready to run the defence on the lines she had urged.

Her investigative efforts were not going to be wasted.

CHAPTER TWENTY-EIGHT

Grainfield Crown Court was over two hundred years old. No surprise, therefore, that it was both dark and cramped. Moreover it gave the impression of having been designed by someone wishing to create a maze of dark oak partitions. Counsel, jury, press and general public all sat in their respective pens. Once the jurors had sat down in theirs only the tops of their heads were visible, giving them the appearance of twelve aunt sallies at a fair stall.

The small dock in the middle of the court had formidable iron spikes on three of its sides and the presiding judge in a position of permanent confrontation at the fourth. He for his part sat on a thronelike chair with a carved canopy above his head and thick burgundy red curtains on either side to protect him from draughts.

The building had been declared an historic monument, though that was small consolation to those who had to work in it. Plans for a new court building had lain around for years, being regularly resurrected and shelved again.

Rosa and Caroline arrived at a side entrance to avoid the posse of press photographers who were waiting outside the main door.

Caroline surrendered to her bail and was taken down to a cell beneath the courtroom to await events.

Rosa went into court and set out her papers. She was relieved to see Ben, a young clerk from her office who had come down to assist her while the trial lasted.

'Make sure nobody has a look at my papers, Ben,' she said. 'I wouldn't put it beyond the press to have a try.'

'Don't worry!' Ben said. 'I'll push anyone's face in if they get funny.'

He was a one-time client of Rosa's who had spent two years in Borstal and on his release had come knocking on the firm's door, asking if there was any chance of a job. Rosa had always felt there was good in him if it were given an opportunity to burgeon and his unexpected arrival on Snaith and Epton's doorstep seemed to present as much a test of her judgement as of Ben's professed determination to go straight. Robin Snaith, her partner, had agreed he should be taken on as office boy and general help. Nine months later there had been no occasion to regret the decision, though there had been times when Rosa held her breath.

'Remember you're not in a boxing ring,' she remarked as she turned to go and look for Counsel. Ben grinned.

'I wouldn't really push anyone's face in,' he said reassuringly. 'Just tell 'em to bugger off.'

As Rosa made her way out of court she spotted Murray Riston and Edward Patching taking their seats in a row reserved for special visitors. She had never met Patching, but had no difficulty in recognising him from descriptions she'd been given. Murray seemed to have aged and looked anything but relaxed as he sat down and stared tensely around him. Catching sight of Rosa he raised a hand in embarrassed salutation.

She found Martin Ainsworth and Paul Elson talking just outside counsel's entrance into court.

'How's Caroline this morning?' Ainsworth asked.

'She'll be all right once things get under way,' Rosa replied.

'I know what you mean. It's like one's first day at boarding school, except a hundred times worse.'

162

As they spoke Beresford Winskip and Bernard Finch, his junior, went past on their way into court. Winskip's wizened clerk brought up the rear carrying his counsel's brief and a pile of law reports.

'He reminds me of a scarred old battle cruiser with attendant destroyer and mine sweeper,' Ainsworth remarked as he observed them. 'I suppose we'd better go in, too, and sort ourselves out.'

Paul Elson gave Rosa a mischievous smile. 'I've only appeared in this court once before and I swear I contracted death watch beetle. If you're my shape, it's sheer hell to sit in.'

A few minutes later Mr Justice Farrow was escorted on to the bench by the High Sheriff of the county and various other dignitaries. After an exchange of bows all round he took his seat and an usher fussily adjusted the heavy curtains either side of his chair.

He had a smooth, youthful face with a small budlike mouth. In fact he looked considerably younger in his wig than without it for his head was totally bald on top. He was generally regarded as a somewhat colourless figure and one whose private life epitomised privacy. He was unmarried and was known to spend the long summer vacation walking alone in the mountains of one country or another. He was also believed to be quite a talented artist, but this was another facet he kept to himself. As somebody in his old chambers had once said, he was colourless in court and virtually invisible out of it. He was courteous, but aloof, and competent in a wholly unobtrusive way. His appointment had occasioned considerable surprise, but he had proved to be a perfectly satisfactory judge, even though the whole of his barristerial life had been spent in the highly specialised field of planning.

'The trouble is,' Ainsworth had remarked to Rosa the previous evening, 'a judge without any known likes or dislikes, and without any personal foibles, is more difficult to adjust to than the other sort.'

'As long as he's not an anti-feminist,' Rosa had said.

'I'd say he was completely neutral, if not neuter.'

With the preliminaries completed, Caroline became the focus of everyone's attention as she came up the narrow steps into the dock, looking as bemused as Alice at the outset of one of her more extravagant adventures.

The clerk read out the indictment and she pleaded not guilty in a quiet, unemotional tone. There followed the empanelling of the jury, in the course of which Martin Ainsworth made use of his right to challenge without cause two of the potential jurors. Each of them appeared startled when asked by the clerk to withdraw. One subsequently looked thunderously angry and the other as if he would remain mystified for the rest of his life.

'Didn't care for the look of either of them,' Ainsworth murmured to Paul Elson. 'The old boy had the air of a dyed in the wool bigot and the younger chap looked as sly as they come.'

Elson nodded. 'It's a good thing to use up a few challenges. Keeps everyone on their toes.'

With the jury sworn, the judge gave a brief nod to prosecuting counsel who rose ponderously to his feet and began his opening speech.

'May it please your lordship; members of the jury, I appear for the crown in this case with my learned friend, Mr Finch and the defendant is represented by my learned friends, Mr Ainsworth and Mr Elson.

'Members of the jury, nobody relishes prosecuting a fellow creature for murder, but it happens to be a public duty which, from time to time, befalls us at the Bar.'

'Hang on to your wig, it's red rhetoric day,' Elson murmured to Ainsworth.

Meanwhile counsel went on, 'But to prosecute a member

164

of our own legal fraternity – a young woman at that – is a peculiarly painful task. Nevertheless it is one from which one mustn't shrink when the evidence points to the commission of a particularly brutal crime.' Counsel paused and surveyed the jury over the top of his half-spectacles. 'On the evening of the second of December last, members of the jury, the staff of the Chief Prosecuting Solicitor held their annual Christmas party at Grainfield Manor. Among those attending were the defendant, Caroline Allard, and the victim of her murderous assault, Thomas Hunsey. The party fulfilled a dual purpose, to say goodbye to the recently retired Chief Prosecuting Solicitor, Edward Patching, and to welcome his successor, Murray Riston. In the course of the evening the defendant left the party and retired to her office, because, as she later said, she had a bad headache and was suffering from emotional stress. She had accepted an invitation to have dinner with the deceased at his home when the party was over, but it is clear she had no desire to do so. The deceased, however, on noticing her absence from the party went in search of her. It is a reasonable inference that he saw her leave the house and followed her out into the winter night and down the drive. Aware that she was being followed, and, indeed, members of the jury, having contrived that she should be, she lured the deceased into the bushes that abut the drive and there murdered him by striking him over the head with a vicious weapon.' Winskip proceeded to describe the weapon and where it came from. 'Thereafter, members of the jury, she returned unseen to her room where she remained until another member of the staff, a Mr Peter Shoreham, found her sitting alone and in the dark. To Mr Shoreham and subsequently to the police, she said she had never left her room. *That* was a lie; the first of several she was to tell the police. Now why, members of the jury, should she lie, if, as she was later to assert, she was innocent of any wrongdoing? The answer, of course, is that she was not innocent and that her lies were a necessary part of her deceit. I shall in due course go into the evidence in detail so that you may judge for yourselves the significance of those lies . . .'

Rosa glanced toward Caroline who was listening to counsel with a puzzled air. From her expression he might have been describing events on the moon in which she had no real interest. Her eyes met Rosa's and Rosa gave her a small encouraging smile, to which she responded with a resigned shrug.

Beresford Winskip had meanwhile become immersed in a detailed description of what was found at the scene of the murder which led him to itemise the pieces of evidence which, he said, clearly incriminated the defendant.

'One of her hairs found on a bush only three yards from where the body lay. The palpable lie about the scratch on her hand and the further lie about not having left her room that evening.' Fixing the jury with a theatrically grave look, he continued, 'May I remind you that we are not dealing with an illiterate or somebody without education. We are dealing with a woman of thirty-five who is a qualified solicitor holding an important post. If such a person tells lies, it is done deliberately and with a specific purpose. Let me remind you further, members of the jury, that the defendant is used to dealing with the police in her daily work. She is not therefore the sort of person to panic at the sight of a policeman. Their presence couldn't possibly upset her unless . . . unless she had something to hide from them.' His tone sank an octave as he went on, 'Her guilt, members of the jury, that's what she had to hide; that's what led her to spin a web of lies and deceit. And that is the sombre inference the prosecution invite you to draw.'

Martin Ainsworth let out a long forensic sigh and cast the jury a look of sympathy. It was intercepted by prosecuting counsel who reacted with a frown of annoyance. Ainsworth sat back pleased with his small diversionary tactic.

'Let me finally say a word on the subject of motive,' Beresford Winskip went on, thrusting out his stomach as though breasting heavy seas. 'In the first place, as his lordship will tell you, the prosecution never have to prove motive. You frequently hear the expression, a motiveless crime. Many crimes are, particularly murders. On the other hand motive is helpful in understanding why something happened. In this case there is no obvious motive and I stress the word obvious.' He drew a deep breath and glared at Rosa whose intent stare he was finding disconcerting. 'The deceased, members of the jury, had a somewhat unsavoury reputation amongst his colleagues as somebody who pried on others. He was a purveyor of gossip and tittle-tattle and apparently derived a perverse pleasure in digging out bits of scandal. In his office was a mirror which enabled him to see everything that went on in the defendant's office. It was clearly rigged up for that purpose. The prosecution suggest that on the day of the murder he witnessed something very much to the defendant's detriment which necessitated her killing him to ensure his silence. Is that so very far-fetched?'

'Are you asking me?' Ainsworth murmured *sotto voce*, causing Winskip to frown angrily.

The jury, who had been listening with increasing mystification, now exchanged one or two puzzled glances.

'What's he supposed to have seen?' an elderly juror wearing a deaf aid said to his neighbour in an aside of bell-like clarity.

'Possibly you're asking yourselves what he might have seen?' prosecuting counsel went on determinedly. 'Well, it's not for me to speculate, but the answer may well become apparent in the course of the trial.'

'Or may not, as the case may be,' Paul Elson muttered scornfully.

A few minutes later Beresford Winskip concluded his

opening and, wrapping his gown around him with an extravagant gesture, sat down.

'Talk about making bricks without straw,' Ainsworth remarked to his junior. 'I wonder he had the nerve even to mention the word motive.'

'I suppose he felt he had to. I wonder what the judge thought.'

'It'd be easier to discover what the Sphinx is thinking.'

The first two witnesses were those pillars of every murder trial. The photographer and the plan drawer, who produced copies of their wares for the jury.

They were soon gone and were followed by George Ives who made his way to the witness box with the reluctant air of an animal about to be branded.

In answer to Winskip's questions he described how he had found Hunsey's body and the action he subsequently took.

'How long have you worked in the prosecuting solicitor's office, Mr Ives?' Ainsworth asked as he rose to cross-examine.

'Twenty-two years, sir.'

'Is it a happy place?'

Ives shifted uncomfortably. 'On the whole, yes,' he said warily.

'But not entirely?'

'I doubt whether anywhere is.'

'Did Mr Riston's appointment have a certain unsettling effect?'

'I don't think I'm the right person to answer that.'

'I'd like you to try, if you would.'

'Every major staff change can have the effect you mention.'

'And Mr Riston's did?'

'Yes.'

'I take it you knew of the deceased's penchant for scandal?'

'Everyone knew.'

'Are you, as chief clerk, responsible for keeping the personal files relating to staff members?'

'Yes.'

'Who, apart from yourself, would have access to them?'

'The Chief Prosecuting Solicitor himself and, in certain circumstances, his deputy.'

'Did Mr Hunsey ever try and persuade you to let him see one of the files?'

George Ives gripped the edge of the witness box and passed his tongue over his lips.

'Yes,' he said in a tense voice. 'And I rebuked him for asking.'

'Whose file was it he wished to see?'

'Do I have to answer that, my lord?'

'I don't see why not,' Mr Justice Farrow said in a fluting voice and waited with pen poised over his notebook.

'It was Mr Riston's.'

'How long ago was that?'

'It was after Mr Riston's appointment as C.P.S. had been announced.'

'Did he tell you why he wanted to examine Mr Riston's personal file?'

'No, because I cut him short as soon as he said what he wanted.'

'Did you tell Mr Riston?'

'Only recently.'

'I take it the file in question related to the period when Mr Riston was previously on the staff?'

'Yes.'

'From your considerable knowledge of the staff, can you suggest any motive Miss Allard may have had for murdering Mr Hunsey?'

'Definitely not.'

'I assume the police have seen both their files?'

'Yes.'

'Thank you, Mr Ives, that's all I wish to ask you.'

Rosa glanced toward where Murray Riston and Edward Patching were sitting like carved idols. Was it her imagination or did Murray now look more haggard than he had before George Ives gave evidence?

'I call Charles Buck,' Winskip announced.

Rosa switched her gaze to Caroline and gave her a quick smile. She had noticed one of the female jurors, a motherly type, cast constant worried glances at Caroline, while a male juror of about Caroline's own age stared at her with unabashed masculine interest. There seemed no doubt that she cut a sympathetic figure in the dock.

Charles Buck took the oath in a firm tone and looked confidently about him. His gaze fell on Caroline, but he showed no sign of recognition. Then he focused his attention on prosecuting counsel.

Questioned by Beresford Winskip about his knowledge of events on the evening of the party, his answers were assured. He personified the witness with nothing to hide and nothing to fear. Moreover, in unlawyerlike fashion he actually answered questions without qualification. Once or twice he threw a coldly dispassionate look in the direction of Edward Patching and Murray Riston, which Ainsworth noted with interest.

When Ainsworth rose to cross-examine Buck ostentatiously polished his spectacles before glancing up to indicate he was ready.

'Would you agree with the last witness that Mr Riston's appointment caused a certain amount of dissension in your office?'

'There was nothing to dissent about. The appointment was made by an outside committee and that was that.'

'Did you yourself apply for the post?'

'You obviously know I did or you wouldn't have asked.'

'So you were disappointed when somebody else was

170

named?'

'Yes, you could say that.'

'Indeed, very angry when you heard the news?'

'Yes,' Buck said, thrusting his chin aggressively forward.

'And have you been on bad terms with Mr Riston ever since he took up his appointment?'

'You could say that, too.'

'And didn't mind who knew it?'

'The situation wasn't of my making.'

'Meaning what?'

'That I wasn't responsible for the appointment of the new C.P.S.'

'Were you surprised when Miss Allard was charged with murder?'

'I'm at an age when nothing surprises me. After all, it seemed plain enough that it was an inside job.'

'You mean that he was killed by someone on the staff?'

'Yes.'

'You have no doubt about that?'

'None.'

'Can you suggest any motive the defendant might have had?'

'No. I assume Hunsey found a skeleton in her cupboard.'

'Might he have found skeletons in a lot of people's cupboards?'

'If he didn't, it wouldn't have been for want of looking.'

'In yours, for example?'

Buck flushed angrily. 'If you know of any, you'll doubtless tell me.'

'Do you recall once telling Miss Allard in the course of conversation that you regarded murder as the one crime of which everyone was capable?'

Buck frowned. 'I may have done. I don't have total recollection of every conversation I've ever had,' he said contemptuously.

'Did you add that you yourself wouldn't hesitate to kill anyone whom you saw as a threat to your security?'

'I've no idea.'

'Might you have said that?'

'Whatever I said, you've certainly taken it out of context.'

'Did *you* murder Tom Hunsey?' Ainsworth asked in a gentle tone.

'Certainly not.'

'Do you agree that you had the opportunity to do so?'

'I don't agree anything of the sort.'

'You've admitted hiding the murder weapon behind a curtain shortly before the crime?'

'I've explained why I did that,' Buck retorted in an increasingly truculent tone.

'Just one final question, Mr Buck. Did you once threaten the deceased with physical violence?'

The witness gaped and appeared to have difficulty in finding words.

'Let me help your recollection,' Ainsworth went on in his most courteous voice. 'Was there an occasion about a year ago when you returned earlier than usual from lunch and found Hunsey going through the drawers of your desk?'

'There was,' Buck said in a strangulated tone.

'Were you extremely angry and did you threaten him with violence?'

'Yes; with every justification.'

'But of course,' Ainsworth remarked sweetly as he sat down.

After the lunch adjournment the afternoon was taken up with medical and scientific witnesses, of whom defending counsel had little to ask. The pathologist agreed with Ainsworth that it was more a man's crime than a woman's, but added hastily he didn't mean a woman could not have committed it.

At half past four, Mr Justice Farrow adjourned the trial

172

until the next morning.

'I don't believe he's said more than two dozen words all day,' Ainsworth remarked to Paul Elson.

'Certainly not much chance of appealing on the grounds of judicial interference,' Elson replied, with a grin.

Beresford Winskip sidled up and fixed Ainsworth with a reproving look.

'I've been pretty patient so far, Martin, but some of your cross-examination has verged on the scandalous. I really ought to have objected.'

'The only reason you didn't object, Berry, was on the principle that give him enough rope and he'll hang his client,' Ainsworth replied cheerfully.

'I've still to learn what your defence is,' Winskip said in a huffed tone.

'I thought it stood out a mile. My client didn't do it, somebody else did.'

Winskip made an impatient gesture. 'I must say I think you went too far in accusing Buck.'

'I didn't accuse him. I merely asked him if he'd done it. After all, he had as much motive as my client, if not more.'

'Well, I'm still wholly in the dark.'

'Tomorrow may bring light,' Ainsworth murmured as he turned away to speak to Rosa.

'How do you think it's gone?' she asked anxiously.

'In hospital language, as well as can be expected.'

'And you still intend to use our secret weapon?'

'Subject to favourable weather! In other words, yes. So you'd better make your arrangements to ensure the witness is here and can be produced to maximum effect.'

CHAPTER TWENTY-NINE

'I didn't really expect to be eating with you this evening,' Caroline remarked as she and Rosa sat down to dinner.

'Why not?' Rosa asked, though she was aware of the answer.

'I thought the judge would probably revoke my bail. It often happens once a trial starts. I'm sure Tarr must have suggested it to Winskip.'

'As a matter of fact, I'd primed Martin Ainsworth in case an application was made, but it doesn't seem to have entered anyone's head. It was obviously up to the judge, but Farrow doesn't seem the type to take initiatives.'

'You've no idea how debilitating it is to sit in a state of complete inactivity for so long,' Caroline said as she handed Rosa a plate of delicious smelling stew.

'You've more than made up for it since we got back.'

'Cooking's the perfect therapy when you're on trial for murder,' Caroline observed with a wry smile.

'Sounds like a T.V. advert.'

After they had finished their meal and washed up, they went into the living-room with two large cups of coffee and spent the rest of the evening playing patience.

Just before they retired upstairs Caroline said with a half-smile, 'And how am I to dress for the second day of the Grainfield stakes?'

'Same as for the first. You looked great. And I don't want

the jury to think you have a different outfit for every day of the trial. It might give them a wrong impression. Natural modesty is always the best bet for anyone in the dock.'

'You really have studied the whole psychology of a trial, haven't you?' Caroline said with amusement.

'You need to when you're a defence lawyer.'

'I'd never even thought of it before now. I suppose you become a bit dehumanised when you spend your life prosecuting.'

The first witness when the trial resumed the next morning was Chief Superintendent Tarr. He was wearing his uniform with a silver crown and star on each shoulder denoting his rank. He also had on his medals, two for police service and two others relating to the time he had spent in the army in Korea and Aden. He took the oath in a resounding tone and waited for prosecuting counsel to fire his first question.

It was nearly an hour before Martin Ainsworth rose to cross-examine.

'I don't quite follow, are you, or is Detective Chief Inspector Russell, the officer in charge of this case?' Ainsworth asked with an innocent air.

'Detective Chief Inspector Russell.'

'But you've played a very active role in the investigation, have you not?'

'I've explained that.'

'Would it be fair to suggest that you've done so from personal choice?'

'I did no more than my duty required.'

'In effect you ran the enquiry?'

'I collaborated in it.'

'And played an extremely prominent part?'

'Yes.'

'Did you early on form the view that the defendant had committed the crime?'

'That was what the evidence indicated.'

'Thereafter did you tend to ignore anything that didn't incriminate her?'

'Certainly not.'

'Are you really telling the court that you kept an open mind?'

'Yes.'

'What about Mr Buck's concealment of the murder weapon?'

'He explained that to my satisfaction.'

'You wanted to believe him?'

'No question of wanting to, I did believe him.'

'It didn't fit your pre-conceived notion not to believe him, did it?'

'It was a loose end that was satisfactorily tied up,' Tarr said disdainfully.

'Have you searched very hard for a motive?'

'Naturally.'

'And the best you can come up with is this fanciful theory of mirrors and a peeping tom?'

'It's not for me to comment.'

'Have you delved into the past in search of a motive?'

'Yes, in so far as I could.'

'At one time did you connect the crime with Mr Riston's appointment?'

'I explored that possibility.'

'Are you quite certain in your own mind that the motive is somewhere to be found in the deceased's taste for scandal?'

'It's the most likely theory.'

'The truth is that you haven't got very far with motive, have you?'

'That's not for me to say. Other witnesses may be able to assist more than I can.'

'We'll doubtless find out,' Ainsworth remarked drily. 'I'd now like to ask you some questions on a different matter. That concerning the murder of Rex Kline.'

Tarr looked sharply at prosecuting counsel who rose slowly to his feet.

'My lord, I don't know how far my learned friend intends to take his questions, but in my submission the murder of Mr Kline has no relevance to the issue before the jury.'

Mr Justice Farrow glanced at Ainsworth with one quizzically raised eyebrow.

'I submit it is extremely relevant, my lord. If your lordship wishes to hear me further it might be better that I should present my argument in the absence of the jury.'

The judge nodded and the jurors filed out of court escorted by the jury bailiff.

After ten minutes of submission and counter-submission, Mr Justice Farrow declared, 'I shall allow your questions, Mr Ainsworth,' and the jury returned.

'I was about to ask you about Mr Kline's murder,' Ainsworth said, once more facing Tarr across the small divide between counsel and witness. 'Is it still under active investigation?'

'Very much so.'

'But nobody has yet been charged?'

'No.'

'Was Mr Kline the father-in-law of Mr Murray Riston?'

'Yes.'

'Was he a guest at the Christmas party?'

'Yes.'

Tarr bit off the monosyllables as if they had a bad taste.

'Would there appear to be a connection between the two crimes?'

'There's no evidence to that effect.'

'Have you sought to connect the defendant with the other murder?'

Tarr hesitated. 'I've naturally explored that possibility.'

'But found no evidence to support it?'

'No-o.'

177

'The very first person you interviewed after discovery of Mr Kline's body was my client, was it not?'

'Yes.'

'Because you assumed the two murders were connected?'

'It seemed possible.'

'Don't you still consider it a possibility?'

'I've said, there's no evidence to connect them,' Tarr said with a note of anger.

'If both murders were committed by the same person, it couldn't have been Miss Allard, could it?'

'I can't answer such a hypothetical question.' It was apparent from his demeanour, however, that he would have liked to unburden himself a great deal further.

Ainsworth sat down and Bernard Finch called Peter Shoreham.

Peter reached the witness box and gave Caroline a fleeting smile. From his expression he might have been about to face a particularly painful session in a dentist's chair. He gripped the sides of the box tightly and constantly moistened his lips. When it came to describing the click of Caroline's door, he did so in a whisper.

When prosecuting counsel resumed his seat, Peter took a deep breath and faced Martin Ainsworth. He blinked stupidly, as Ainsworth said in an almost offhand manner, 'I have no questions to ask this witness.'

As he said later to his wife, 'There I was, expecting a bullet between the eyes and all I got was a squirt of water.'

'I now call Detective Sergeant Baxter,' Winskip said, casting Ainsworth a wary glance.

Martin Ainsworth rose to his feet as if activated by a button.

'My lord, it's my submission that the evidence of this witness is wholly irrelevant and should not be admitted.' Once more the jury trooped out, leaving defending counsel to address the judge. 'As I understand it, my lord, this witness is being called to prove some sort of motive against my client, the suggestion being that the deceased, by means of his rigged up mirror saw her in possession of cocaine . . . It is difficult to conceive of a more tenuous connection than that between a missing packet of the drug and the defendant's improper possession of it. Moreover, how you can identify cocaine by looking into a mirror passes all belief. If the deceased saw anything at all, and that in itself is pure speculation, how could he possibly tell what the substance was? It might have been baking powder or a cosmetic or almost any other powder you care to think of . . . I ask your lordship to exclude this evidence as having no probative value.'

'Despite my learned friend's scorn,' Winskip said as he heaved himself to his feet to reply, 'this officer's evidence is important and relevant and helps to indicate motive. I accept, of course, that it will be for the jury to decide what weight they give it, but that's another matter . . . In my submission, it should be admitted.'

Both counsel looked forward toward the judge who said in his fluting tones, 'In my view Detective Sergeant Baxter's evidence should not be heard. Its prejudicial effect far outweighs any probative value it might have and I therefore rule against its admission.'

Rosa glanced toward where Tarr was now sitting and saw his look of anger. She knew how hard he had fought to have that particular piece of evidence adduced. Well, it served him right.

Detective Chief Inspector Russell was the last prosecution witness. He gave his evidence in a quiet, subdued tone and was plainly uncomfortable under cross-examination, during which he studiously avoided looking in the direction of his Chief Superintendent.

'Tell me, chief inspector, do *you* think there must be a connection between the two murders?' Ainsworth asked.

'There's no evidence to support that, sir.'

'No evidence? What do you call the fact that they both attended the same party and were murdered within ten days of each other? Is that mere coincidence?'

'Mr Kline's murder has us baffled at the moment, sir,' Russell said defensively.

'Be honest, Mr Russell, wasn't your immediate reaction on learning of Mr Kline's death that there must be a connection between the two crimes?'

'That was certainly my initial reaction,' he replied with an unhappy air.

'Isn't it still your opinion?'

'We've no evidence . . .'

But Martin Ainsworth had already sat down.

'That, my lord, is the case for the prosecution,' Winskip announced with what sounded like a sigh of resignation.

Ainsworth was on his feet again.

'I shall be calling the defendant, my lord, and at least one other witness.'

CHAPTER THIRTY

As Rosa watched Caroline make her way from dock to
witness box she recalled a sermon her father had once
preached. Most of them she found regrettably unmemor-
able, but this one had always stayed in her mind. It had been
on the subject of sympathy and he had reminded his
congregation that the word meant 'suffering with', which
seemed to epitomise her feelings at this particular moment.
She felt she was sharing Caroline's ordeal as she took the oath
and faced Martin Ainsworth.

'Did you murder Tom Hunsey?' he asked as his opening
question.

'No,' she said in a firm tone.

Rosa breathed a sigh of relief. It was not that she had
feared Caroline might say 'yes' and burst into tears, but the
unexpectedness of the question could have caught her off
balance so that her answer carried less than conviction.

'Did you have any motive for murdering him?'

'None.'

'On the other hand, were you close by when he was killed?'

'Yes, I was,' Caroline said quietly with a small shiver.

'Please tell the court exactly what happened.'

The jury gave her their full attention as she retailed the
events of the fateful evening, showing an interest that hadn't
always been apparent during the trial.

Without prompting she admitted her lies to the police and

explained why she had told them.

'I'm afraid I was under a considerable emotional strain that evening,' she said.

'I think you must tell the jury the cause of it,' Ainsworth broke in.

She threw him a reproachful look and bit nervously at her lip.

'I had had an affair with Mr Riston when he was previously on the staff and . . . and, well I suppose I'd never really got over it. His return to Grainfield as C.P.S. aroused a lot of painful memories.'

'Was there anything special about the party to upset you?'

'Only that it was approaching Christmas and the first time I'd seen him socially since his return. I felt suddenly overwhelmed.'

Rosa glanced at Murray, who was staring at Caroline with a fraught expression. He had the air of a drowning man whose past life was being remorselessly played back to him.

'Anything else I ought to ask her?' Ainsworth whispered to Rosa. She shook her head and, after a brief word with Paul Elson, Ainsworth sat down.

Winskip rose with the majesty of a missile off its launching pad.

'You're quite adept at telling lies when it suits you?' he said in a heavily sardonic tone.

'I don't make a habit of it,' Caroline said in a voice little above a whisper.

'You did on the occasion with which we're concerned?'

'I've admitted telling lies then and I've told the court why.'

'Would it be fair to say that you've only admitted your lies because you had no alternative?'

'No, I don't think it would,' Caroline said with a slight frown.

'It was a tactical decision to abandon them, wasn't it?'

'When I realised how foolish I'd been, I was anxious to tell

182

the truth.'

'But you've had many opportunities of telling the truth, why didn't you do so much earlier?'

'Because Chief Superintendent Tarr didn't make it easy for me.'

'So it was all his fault you told lies, is that what you're saying?'

'No, I'm not saying that at all.'

'Why couldn't you have told him the truth on one of the occasions he interviewed you?'

'Because he'd made it clear he thought I was guilty and I felt that whatever I said would be turned against me.'

'Are you saying that he treated you unfairly?'

'He'd convinced himself of my guilt and was determined to charge me. Once he'd bailed me under the Magistrates Courts Act he had to do so or lose face. And Mr Tarr is not somebody who willingly contemplates losing face.'

'Are you seriously suggesting that a chief superintendent of police turned a murder investigation into a personal vendetta?'

'I'm merely saying that he convinced himself of my guilt and nothing I could say was going to shake his belief.'

'Would you agree that your present story shows all the signs of having been carefully shaped to account for every bit of evidence that incriminates you?'

'It's not been shaped, as you put it. It's the truth.'

'Isn't it a remarkable coincidence that, if you're to be believed, Hunsey was murdered almost at your feet by an unknown third person?'

'It's what happened.'

'It's totally implausible, isn't it?'

'It's the truth.'

'I suggest the truth, Miss Allard, is that it was you who killed him?'

Caroline shook her head vigorously. 'No . . . no.'

'Are you still telling lies?' Winskip said and sat down.

As Caroline returned to the dock, Ainsworth leaned forward and spoke to Rosa.

'Is she here?' he asked.

'Yes. Ben fetched her. She's waiting in the car.'

'Good!' Rising to his feet and addressing nobody in particular, he announced in a loud voice, 'I call Mrs Patching.'

CHAPTER THIRTY-ONE

Rosa craned her head to catch Murray Riston's aghast look, while Edward Patching wore the stunned air of somebody for whom reality has suddenly dissolved. Two rows behind them Charles Buck sat like an expressionless Buddha.

The woman who came into the witness box and took the oath was in her fifties. She was wearing a purple skirt and jacket and her autumn-tinted hair rose up in lacquered waves and looked as stiff as a stale meringue. She had a thin face and an unforgiving mouth.

She took off one glove in order to hold the testament and take the oath. Afterwards she pulled it carefully back on again.

'Is your name Jean Patching?' Ainsworth asked.

'It is.'

'And are you the divorced wife of Edward Patching?'

'I am.'

'Which of you divorced the other?'

'I divorced him on the grounds of his adultery with one of his secretaries,' she said in a contemptuous tone.

'When was that?'

'Four years ago.'

'And was a settlement made in your favour?'

'Yes.'

'Did your husband keep up the alimony payments?'

'No.'

'With what result?'

'I threatened to take him back to court.'

'Was he still C.P.S. at the time?'

'Very much so.'

'Do you recall an occasion in October a year after the divorce when he came to see you?'

'I do. We had an acrimonious meeting, at the end of which I gave him an ultimatum. Namely, that if I didn't receive every penny that was due to me within one month he'd have to face some disagreeable consequences. He had pleaded poverty and said he was still paying off the costs of the divorce action, but I'd heard it all before and was unmoved. I may say he left my house in a considerably chastened mood.'

'What was the next thing that happened?'

'I received a cheque from him for £10,000.'

'Were you surprised?'

'Extremely surprised, as he'd told me he'd been trying to borrow money without any success.'

'Do you know from whom he'd tried to borrow?'

'From Mr Kline.'

'What did you do with the cheque?'

'I paid it in to my account without delay. And because I was intrigued to know how he'd suddenly come by such a large sum of money, I made some discreet enquiries.'

'Where?'

'At the bank where we both still had accounts. I had a particular friend there and had a private word with him on the side.'

'What did you discover?'

'That my ex-husband had recently paid in a cheque for £10,000 drawn in his favour by Mr Kline.'

'When was that?'

'It was in November.'

'Can you relate it to another event?'

'It was about a week after a road accident in which a cyclist

had been killed by a hit and run motorist.' She gave
Ainsworth a quietly triumphant look. 'And I can tell you
something further. I later learnt that on the evening in
question Mr Kline had been my ex-husband's guest at an
official dinner in Portsmouth.'

'Did you ever meet Tom Hunsey?'

'Several times.'

'When was the last occasion?'

'About a week before my ex-husband's retirement as
C.P.S. He came to see me.'

'Did he come and see you about something specific?'

'Yes, he believed I could help him solve a mystery.'

'What mystery?'

'Who the hit and run motorist was.'

'And could you?'

'I like to think so,' she said, swinging round and staring
with a mixture of bitterness and contempt at the ashen-faced
Edward Patching.

'No . . . no,' he gasped. 'It wasn't me driving . . .'

The next moment he had crashed to the floor in a dead
faint.

CHAPTER THIRTY-TWO

It was several minutes before Patching could be extricated and assisted out of court by Detective Chief Inspector Russell and others. Neither Murray Riston nor Charles Buck made any attempt to follow him.

Throughout the turmoil and the usher's futile cries of 'silence in court', Mr Justice Farrow had remained impassive. He now turned toward counsel and said, 'I'll adjourn for twenty minutes, at the end of which time counsel may like to come and see me in my room.'

'Is that a command?' Paul Elson enquired after the judge had left the bench.

'As near as he'll ever get to one,' Ainsworth commented.

'What the hell are we going to do now?' Winskip asked, as he slid along the pew to where Ainsworth was sitting.

'I trust that when we go and see the judge you'll be telling him that you're throwing in your hand.'

'I can't do that! I mean, I haven't even cross-examined your witness.'

'Think it'll do you much good?'

'If you ask me, that woman's a bitch of the first order.'

'I'm inclined to agree, though I'm probably being a bit unchivalrous in the circumstances.'

'Most of her evidence was totally inadmissible.'

'How can you say that when it's as good as secured my client's acquittal!'

'Anyway, what are we going to say to the judge?'

'I suggest we ask him to adjourn until tomorrow morning, by which time you'll have been able to consult the police and those instructing you and I shall confidently expect you to be in a position to inform the court that the prosecution is no longer asking the jury to convict.'

A few minutes later when they reached the judge's room, they found Mr Justice Farrow, wig off, sipping a cup of herbal tea. He listened to what Beresford Winskip had to say and nodded his acquiescence. On returning to court he said he was sure the jury would understand the desirability of adjourning in the light of the somewhat unusual situation that had arisen. Meanwhile he advised them not to jump to conclusions, but to keep their own counsel until the trial resumed.

When Rosa and Caroline arrived at court the next day, they had to fight their way into the building. Word of 'sensational developments' (to quote the most used cliché) had spread and appeared to have drawn reporters and television crews to Grainfield from far and wide.

Eventually they reached the sanctuary of a small conference room where they had arranged to meet Martin Ainsworth and Paul Elson.

Caroline, who had scarcely had any sleep the previous night, looked worn out and smothered frequent yawns. She was obviously on edge as, one way or another, the final stages of the trial drew closer.

'It's like a siege outside,' Ainsworth remarked when he and Elson arrived.

'What's the news?' Rosa asked anxiously.

'I've had only the briefest word with Berry Winskip, but the prosecution is definitely throwing in the towel. Apart from telling me that, he was unusually tight-lipped.'

There was a knock on the door and it opened to reveal Detective Chief Inspector Russell with a sea of craning heads

189

behind him. He stepped inside closing the door quickly behind him.

'I'm having the lobby cleared so that you won't have to run the gauntlet getting into court,' he said. 'Afterwards I'll arrange for you to leave by a rear entrance and will have a police car ready. If you let me have your car keys, Miss Epton, I'll have it picked up and brought to you. May I suggest that you don't return immediately to Miss Allard's cottage, as it, too, will be under siege. Is there anything else you want to know?'

'All I've been told is that the prosecution is dropping its case,' Ainsworth said. 'We don't know the background to the decision.'

Russell gave a small, weary smile. 'I suppose Mrs Patching's evidence is the background,' he remarked. 'You saw what effect it had on her husband. It almost disembowelled him. It would take a psychologist to explain all the changes of mood he's been through since we carried him out of court yesterday. At one time we couldn't stop him talking. He was like a burst water main, words simply gushed out of him. He's now admitted both murders. Apparently in the course of the party Hunsey hinted he'd found out that Rex Kline was the hit and run driver and that Mr Patching was his passenger. They were on their way back from Portsmouth at the time. Later Kline lent or gave him £10,000 in exchange for his silence about the accident. Incidentally, Mr Patching was most insistent that it wasn't a bribe. Something else for a psychologist to explain,' Russell observed drily. 'Fearful that Hunsey in his slightly tipsy state might speak his thoughts to others, Mr Patching followed him outside when he saw him go off in search of Miss Allard, having first armed himself with Alec's cosh which he had seen Mr Buck conceal behind a curtain.' Russell paused and gave an exhausted sigh. 'It appears that Mr Kline's suspicions were aroused and a few days later they met secretly in the golf shelter to discuss their common situation. Nothing was resolved, but it's quite clear that each was only interested in achieving his own security. I don't know whether it ever actually occurred to Mr Kline to kill Mr Patching, but certainly the reverse applied. Their second meeting was at Rex Kline's suggestion and Mr Patching went prepared. As long as they both lived, each remained the other's hostage . . .' He looked at Rosa with a half-sad, half-admiring look. 'You've certainly shown us up, Miss Epton.'

'Will Mr Tarr be in court this morning?' she asked.

He shook his head. 'No, he has other matters to attend to.' Glancing at his watch he went on quickly, 'It's time we went into court. I'll just make sure the way's clear.'

As soon as Mr Justice Farrow took his seat, Beresford Winskip informed him with the appropriate amount of lawyer's circumlocution that the prosecution didn't wish to proceed further.

Turning toward the jury, the judge directed them to return a verdict of not guilty. When this had been done, he added in a sudden burst of unwonted words, 'A bizarre end to a wholly remarkable case, which I'm sure you will always remember.'

Detective Chief Inspector Russell insisted on accompanying Rosa and Caroline when they were driven away from court.

'What I can't understand is why Mrs Patching never approached the police herself, seeing the relish she showed in the witness box in hammering one nail after another into her husband's coffin,' he remarked as they headed out of Grainfield.

'She might have done if she'd been in possession of all the facts,' Rosa said.

'But she knew the hit and run incident coincided with her ex-husband and Mr Kline having an evening out together and once Hunsey had been to see her . . .'

'She only learnt the two men had been together that evening very much later.'

'I wonder how she found out.'

'I told her,' Rosa said in a matter of fact tone.

'You mean you'd dug that out?'

'Yes; as well as how a lot of other people spent that same evening.'

Russell was pensive for a while. 'You don't want to join the police, do you, Miss Epton?' he enquired.

In due course Caroline sold her cottage and severed her remaining ties with Grainfield. She received a sum of money by way of compensation, but as she had said all along, Tarr had managed to assassinate her professionally. He himself was forced into early retirement and also left the district.

Caroline went off to visit a cousin who farmed in New Zealand and, apart from occasional postcards, Rosa didn't hear from her for over two months. Then a letter arrived.

Dearest Rosa, it read. *Only now do I feel able to sit down and write you a letter of true gratitude. I was an awkward, unhelpful client, not to mention a wayward friend, but all the while you were wonderful and I shall always be indebted to you. My shattered life still lies around my feet in tiny pieces and more days than not I wonder if I'll ever be able to put it together again. I'm not sure it's a good thing to have so much time to think. Here on Oliver's farm I'm surrounded by kindness and sheep, but one day I must bestir myself and take an initiative. What do you suggest?*

Your loving and ever grateful friend,

Caroline.

Rosa wrote back by return; a postcard with a picture of a red London bus. It read:

Why not come and join Snaith and Epton? Love, Rosa.